Cupcakes

and

Corpses

POLLY HOLMES

Western Australia

COPYRIGHT

Published by Gumnut Press

Copyright © 2019 Polly Holmes

ISBN: 978-0-6485325-4-5

Edited by Nina S. Gooden
(www.greenteaandpinkink.com)

Cover by Mariah Sinclair (www.thecovervault.com)

DEDICATION

To all cupcake bakers around the world.

Thank you

ALSO BY POLLY HOLMES

The Cupcake Series

Cupcakes and Cyanide

Cupcakes and Curses

Cupcakes and Corpses

Mistletoe and Murder

Publishers Stocking Polly Holmes Books

Amazon

Gumnut Press

Novella Distribution

Chapter One

CASSIDY MCCORRSON SEARCHED her purse for another two-dollar coin, her mind racing through the meticulous tasks she had scheduled for the day. Standing in line at the Tea 4 Two Café, Cassidy knew in her heart there weren't enough hours in the day to meet the deadline of her current design project. With less than forty-eight hours before her clients returned, she'd never know why she agreed to redesign and decorate an entire lounge room, three weeks before Christmas.

While her sisters' claims to fame were delicious, award-winning cupcakes, Cassidy's passion was interior design. It was the same passion as her mother's. She'd been back in Ashton Point a little under a month and already her schedule was off the charts. She'd barely had time to settle back into living with her two older sisters, Clair and Charlotte.

Thinking about her work was enough to get her mind buzzing. The thrill of making someone's dream home come true never grew old. The expression on her client's faces when she unveiled her creations warmed her heart.

I guarantee you, Mr and Mrs Jacobs, you're going to love your new lounge room.

Who could have known that when she returned from the US, her skills would be in such demand? By all accounts, she should still be in New York celebrating a white Christmas. The sudden sting of betrayal hit her hard.

The sweet aroma of caramel and chocolate sifting through the café tantalised her nostrils. *Mmmm…chocolate.*

Margarete's steaming, chocolaty concoction would go nicely with her sister's strawberry and cherry cupcakes, which Cassidy had picked up from CC's Simply Cupcakes on the way. She licked her lips, salivating at the thought of Charlotte's mouth-watering cupcakes. She was so lost in the world of sugary treats that she jumped and her heart skipped a beat when her name rang out across the café.

"Won't be long, Cassidy," Margarete called, her cornflour-blue eyes peering over the top of the coffee machine. "We're a little busier than normal this morning. Got to love tourist season."

"No problem," Cassidy said graciously with a smile. *But please hurry, my cupcakes are missing me.*

She gazed around at the excitement on the faces of the eager customers. With Christmas only weeks away, the town buzz was electrifying. Cassidy did love this time of year in Ashton Point, especially when she got to spend it with her sisters.

A giggle from within her belly worked its way up to her throat. They hadn't exactly given her the warm homecoming she'd expected. The corner of her lip pulled into a smile as she remembered the sight of Clair, poised and ready to strike, her baseball bat held high enough to kiss her earlobe.

"Freeze or you're dead meat," Clair barked from the hallway. Cassidy had jumped in fright at the sharpness of Clair's voice. She'd almost dropped her cucumber and cheese sandwich. It's not like she was a raving lunatic who had broken in while they were at the gala dinner just to make a sandwich.

A sharp, disgruntled voice boomed from the door of the café, bringing Cassidy crashing back to reality. "Would you mind telling me what you think you're doing, Miss McCorrson?"

The icy tone chilled Cassidy to the core. *What the... It can't be. I must be dreaming.*

She spun and her stomach dropped. Christina Jacobs, owner of the local newspaper, *The Chronicle*, stood blocking the entrance in her perfectly tailored, black cashmere dress suit. Her glacial gaze drilled into Cassidy.

"Christina Jacobs, what are you doing here?"

Audible gasps rocked the interior of the café and all inquisitive eyes were cemented squarely on Christina. Her blonde curls bounced across her stiff shoulders as she sashayed her way across the wooden floor, her hips swaying like a see-saw as she went.

"Oh, Cassidy, dear. You shouldn't believe everything you hear, especially in a town like Ashton Point. They do say you can't keep a good woman down. In the world of today, it's not what you know, but who you know." Christina smirked and swung her guilty leer around the café.

Rage burned deep in Cassidy's belly. "Are you kidding me? I hope you don't think you can waltz back into town and make my sister's life hell again."

"There's one version of the truth and then there's mine."

Margarete's silky voice called across the café. "Cassidy, your coffee is ready."

Saved by the bell. "Coming," Cassidy called over her shoulder. Glaring at Christina's stony face, she said, "If you'll excuse me, I need to be somewhere else. Anywhere else."

Christina thrust her hands on her hips. "If by 'anywhere else,' you mean my parents' retreat, then it looks like I'm back just in time."

Cassidy felt the blood drain from her face. "What's *that* supposed to mean?"

Christina's sarcastic tone sent shivers up Cassidy's spine. "Mother didn't tell you, did she?"

"Tell me what?" Silence fell on the tense café and Cassidy held her breath, praying a storm wasn't about to strike where they stood. No such luck.

"While my parent's retreat is attached to the side of my house, I'm still the owner of the property. Mother always wanted to redesign the interior, but it was my idea to make the renovations a part of their anniversary present. I'm back and I'm in charge now. I can't believe what you've done to my house."

The jingling of the bells over the café door signalling a customer entry was a distant sound, compared to the whine of Christina's voice. Cassidy raised an eyebrow and asked, "You're in charge? Where are your parents?"

"The Caribbean, I think. Another part of my anniversary present. They were already in Sydney on holiday. I just extended it a few weeks," Christina said with a smirk. "Didn't they tell you?"

Cassidy shook her head, the excitement she'd felt a moment ago drained from her body.

"I expected a masterpiece when I walked into their retreat. Not a catastrophic nightmare, which is what you've delivered." Christina's words slashed Cassidy's heart like a samurai sword slicing silk. "I thought you were an award-winning interior designer. I guess that's why my mother hired you. From the state of the lounge room, the only award you'll be receiving is from the back of a Corn Flakes packet."

Oh no, she didn't just dis' my talent. "I'll have you know, my talents are highly sought after. *And* your mother absolutely loved the fabrics I chose for the curtains. They're the current trend in New York. My mother recently used that exact design in several high-end client apartment revamps."

Christina folded her arms across her chest, pushing her voluptuous cleavage straight into Cassidy's view. "She was just being polite. That's the sort of woman she is. My mother may have hired you, but I'm firing you."

Cassidy's insides were sizzling like a witch's cauldron. "What?"

Scattered, rumbling murmurs between customers began to just barely penetrate the animated discussion. She sucked in a deep lungful of air and slid her fingers around her coffee. Tingles slowly flooded her palms as the warmth spread through her hands.

"If you're not satisfied with my work, that's fine. Just pay me the balance of what is owed and I'll have my equipment out of the house within the hour."

"Ha, as if. I refuse to pay for shoddy work. You'll not get a cent out of me or my mother," Christina snapped. "And don't think of bothering her while she's on her cruise. I made sure they weren't to be disturbed unless it was an emergency."

Detective Anderson cleared his throat and stepped forward. "Ladies. The last thing I expected to find when I came in for my morning coffee was you two going at it like two spoilt children fighting over the last chocolate bar. What will the tourists think? It's probably best to end this conversation now before it gets too out of hand."

"We have a contract," Cassidy said her voice raised an octave. "And it states that the balance, $17,500, must be paid with or without the work finished. You cannot refuse to pay."

"I can and I will. My lawyer is Christopher Linnell." Christina paused, flicking her blonde ringlets over her shoulder. "You may have heard of him?"

The name sounded vaguely familiar. Cassidy pursed her lips as Christina's droning voice pounded her mind.

"He's a high-class lawyer in Sydney. His clientele is some of the most well-known people in Australia. Christopher will be in Ashton Point at the end of the week and I'm sure he'll find a loophole in that contract. And if I see you anywhere near my house—and that includes my parents' retreat—so help me, there will be hell to pay."

Before Cassidy had a chance to respond, Detective Anderson stepped between the two women, the snappy tone in his voice startling Cassidy. "Ladies, please. This is hardly the time or the place for this type of discussion."

Cassidy caught the frowning gaze of some tourists sitting over by the window and felt her cheeks redden with embarrassment. "I guess you're right," Cassidy said, sidestepping both of them. "But this isn't over, not by a long shot. I will get the money owed to me, one way or another," she said.

Under the onslaught of inquisitive eyes, she turned and left.

Chapter Two

"I CAN'T BELIEVE nerve of that woman," Cassidy said, pacing the kitchen of CC's Simply Cupcakes, her blood boiling. She popped the last bite of her strawberry-cherry cupcake into her mouth, devouring it in seconds. "How dare she fire me... *Me*. And now I'm $17,500 out of pocket. She wouldn't know a great design if she tripped over and fell face first into it."

It hadn't taken Cassidy more than fifteen minutes to make it back to CC's Simply Cupcakes. The town gossip vine was on fire and the news of her vocal disagreement with Christina beat her to the mark.

"Don't worry about the money, Cassidy. Charlotte and I can help out 'til something comes along. The business is doing well and as soon as I get CC's Cupcake Haven up and running in the old Sweets Mansion, things will be even better. Besides, the way you are transforming that old place into a modern-day, vintage-chic masterpiece will be breathtaking. The people of this town will be lining up to have you design their houses."

Charlotte frowned. "Clair's right. You are amazing. But I did warn you, she was a piece of work." She continued to pipe lemon icing on vanilla cupcakes in swirls of sugary delight.

"Yeah, I know you did, but I was dealing with her parents. I never thought I'd have to contend with Christina. It's hard to believe they're from the same gene pool."

Clair huffed, punching the keys on her laptop as she spoke. "That woman certainly knows how to make your life a living hell. I bet she's looking to inflict more havoc across our beautiful town. You'd do well to steer clear of her."

"If it weren't for Christina, you may never have met Mason Hapworth," Charlotte piped up. "And we all know that you're head over heels for him. Especially since he moved to Ashton Point to be at your beck and call."

"Charlotte," Clair said, her word coming out in a squeal.

"She's right, Clair. It's so obvious you're smitten with him. And he is with you." A pang of resentment embedded itself deep in Cassidy's belly. Two months ago, she'd been the same. In love with Todd Williams, the man she'd thought she'd spend the rest of her life with.

How wrong was I? Just goes to show you can't judge a book by its cover.

On the outside, Todd had been everything she dreamed of. Pristine and perfect. Gorgeous, with a body to die for, the Hugh Jackman *Wolverine* type. He was a Wall Street tycoon who'd promised her the world. His insides were a different story. He was a cunning, cheating manipulator who was only interested in climbing up the corporate ladder. With not a care in the world of who he crushed in the process.

"Earth to Cassidy," Clair called, snapping her fingers. "Where did you go? We lost you there for a second."

Her eyes caught her sisters' concerned gazes. They were clearly waiting for an explanation. She swallowed the knot of regret in her throat. "Oh, sorry. I was just thinking about that woman. I swear she's pure evil."

Charlotte opened the oven a smidgen to check her latest batch of chocolate-caramel cupcakes. The scintillating aroma oozed out, teasing Cassidy's nostrils. "Really, Charlotte... Did you have to do that? You know chocolate and caramel is one of my favourites. Now I want one of those, even though I'm stuffed from the ones I ate earlier."

A hearty giggle erupted from Charlotte's lips. "Oh, I have missed you. Sorry, it's Pierre's day off and Suzi will be out soon to fill the display cabinet with them before the lunchtime rush."

"So, that's a no?" Cassidy asked. "I'm not so sure about my tastebuds, but my waistline will thank you. I did miss your superb cooking skills while I was in New York. They had a cupcake stall just around the corner from Mum and Dad's apartment building, but their cupcakes couldn't hold a candle to yours."

Clair and Charlotte gazed toward each other at the mention of New York. Clair bit her lip and frowned, as if wanting to say something but unsure of how to word it. "Do you think you're ready to tell us why you came back early? The last time we spoke to Mum she said you had decided to stay for a white Christmas."

Mortification struck and her chest tightened. *No, absolutely not.* If she told them about Todd, they'd probably be on the next plane to New York to beat him to a pulp. Thank goodness she hadn't fessed up to her parents that she'd fallen in love with a jerk. "I told you guys. I just felt I'd overstayed my welcome with Mum and Dad."

"That's why you were moping around the house... Because Mum and Dad were cramping your style?" Charlotte asked, taking the baking tray from the oven.

Cassidy felt heat work its way up her neck to her cheeks. *Great, now not only will my nose be as long as Pinocchio's, but I'll also look like a beetroot ready to burst.* She picked up her bag and threw it over her shoulder.

"What is with the third degree? If you remember, I was suffering jet lag and was sleeping most of the day. You've both been to visit them, you know what it's like." She turned and headed toward the door, masking the warm blush of her cheeks. "Now that I've got a bit more time, I'll head over to the Sweets place to work on my designs. The refit is coming along nicely, but there are a few things I'm still working on. Then I'm going to head into Watson's Creek to the fabric shop to look at some samples so don't wait up."

Sweat rolled down the side of Cassidy's temple as she flung off her sheet. The sweltering summer nights had kicked in early. "That'll teach me to forget to turn the air-conditioner on before I go to bed." She'd tossed and turned most of the night, the conversation with Christina replaying in her head like a scratched vinyl record. Glistening beams of sunlight streaked through the window, warming her bedroom, and her bedside clock hadn't even struck 8 a.m.

Christina's spiteful words left the bitter taste of uncertainty in her mouth. She hadn't let on to her sisters how much Christina's harsh words had shattered her confidence. Her mother had spotted Cassidy's talent for interior design at an early age, nurtured and developed it until she followed in her footsteps with a Bachelor of Design Arts in interior design.

From the state of the lounge room, the only award you'll be receiving is from the back of a Corn Flakes packet.

"Ahhhhhh," she screamed into her pillow, letting all her frustration bleed out. She sat upright, throwing her pillow toward the foot of the bed. "Take that, Christina Jacobs. I'll show you how much talent I have. People in this town love my designs and when they see the amazing design I've done on CC's Cupcake Haven, they'll be blown away and your comment will be a distant memory." By the time she'd showered, dressed and headed out to the kitchen, a sense of ease flowed through her body.

"Morning," she said to Clair as she entered the kitchen. Her gaze scanned the room for Charlotte.

"Don't bother, she's gone for a run. Something about trying to get in shape before Christmas so she doesn't have to count her calories when all the yummy Christmas treats come out."

"Since when did she start counting calories?" Cassidy asked popping a Caramelito pod in the Nespresso machine. "Her figure looks fine to me." Her belly grumbled as the smell of barely-cooked toast played havoc on her senses.

"Since Liam emerged on the scene." Clair fiddled, squeezing the toaster back in the cupboard between the blender and the sandwich press.

Cassidy frowned. "Appears I missed all the fun while I was away. I come home and both my sisters are dating."

Liam had arrived in Ashton Point a few months back to be Lincoln's best man at the wedding of the year. The wedding that almost destroyed CC's Simply Cupcakes. Charlotte had been accused of poisoning her cupcakes with cyanide and murdering poor Mr Hutson. A preposterous accusation. Who in their right mind would kill someone with the tools of their trade?

"I haven't been able to spend much time with Liam since I've been back but he seems really charming and is obviously besotted with Charlotte. I'm really happy for her."

Clair's gaze locked onto Cassidy's and her throaty laugh filled the kitchen. "Besotted? Sounds like you belong in Sherwood Forest with Robin Hood."

Cassidy opened her mouth to speak but before she could, the belch of the doorbell rang throughout the house, cutting her words short. "Are you expecting anyone?"

Clair's eyebrows creased as she shook her head. "No. Maybe Charlotte forgot her key when she went for her run. I'll get it," she said as she moseyed toward the door.

Cassidy closed her eyes and savoured the warm, frothy liquid as it trickled down the back of her throat. *Whoever invented coffee should be given a medal.* She waited for the caffeine to hit her bloodstream.

Cassidy's body tensed and her spine straightened as the testy tone in Clair's voice boomed down the hallway. "Hey, you can't barge into our house for no reason."

Anderson's heels scraped the tiled floor before stopping in the centre of the kitchen. His eyelids narrowed at Cassidy as she stood by the table, steaming coffee in hand. "I have a reason. I'm glad you're here, Cassidy. You're just the McCorrson I was looking for."

"Me?" Cassidy asked, her gaze shooting from Detective Anderson to his offsider, Robert Loughlin. "Hi, Robert," she said, a cautious smile edging her upper lip.

"Morning, Cassidy," he said, squirming. He looked as uncomfortable and she felt.

Detective Anderson pulled a plastic evidence bag from his right inside pocket and held it up for all to see. "Does this look familiar?"

Cassidy felt the blood drain from her face and a sense of foreboding hit her square in the gut. Her words froze in the back of her throat. *Yes. My pink, Valentino lace trim scarf, but what's it doing in an evidence bag?*

Anderson grew impatient and took a step closer. "I'll ask you again. Do you recognise this piece of clothing?"

She could almost hear her heart beating in the silent room as all three stood there, waiting for her answer. Slowly she nodded. "Yes, I recognise that scarf or one like it."

"So, you admit it's yours?" Robert asked, moving to stand beside Detective Anderson.

Cassidy folded her arms and glared in Robert's direction. "I said I recognised it. I never said it was mine."

"It's been a long night and I'm in no mood for games, just answer the question," Anderson snapped.

Cassidy's eyes widened and she gripped her coffee cup so hard her fingertips were turning white.

"I am answering your questions." *You pompous busybody. No need to be rude about it.*

"So, you're denying you own a scarf like this one?" he asked dropping the bag on the kitchen table.

"I'm not denying anything. It looks familiar because I own one similar. I bought mine in New York but you can get them online. Anyone else in this town could have ordered one. It's a very popular scarf this season." Her heart lurched at the look of panic on her sisters' face.

"Why all the questions, Detective?" Clair asked.

He rubbed his five o'clock shadow, his forehead frowning into a monobrow. "I'm afraid this scarf was found wrapped around the neck of a body we found early this morning."

"Oh, how awful." Her chest tightened and his words were like a punch to her gut with a steel crowbar. "Who was it?"

"Christina Jacobs."

The girls exchanged glances as a sudden chill filled the room. Cassidy swallowed the lump in her throat. "And you think because I own one just like it, I did it?" They paused, their silence a confirmation of her guilt. "Are you serious? That is the most preposterous accusation I've ever heard."

"That may be so." Detective Anderson nodded his head toward the door. "We'd still like for you to come down the station for questioning."

"What?" The girls blurted in unison.

Cassidy willed herself to stay calm but it wasn't easy with a certain Detective needling at her focus. *Who does he think he is? Sherlock Holmes?* "That scarf could belong to anyone and it's not like Christina had a lot of friends in town."

"You've got to be kidding me," Clair said. Detective Anderson grimaced at her frustrated tone. "Is this a ritual for you now? Every time you find a corpse, you assume it is one of us. First, Charlotte, then me, and now Cassidy."

"Is it my fault that every time a body turns up you girls are linked to it in some way?" he asked, his eyes darkening.

Robert's deep tone calmed the storm brewing in her belly. "Cassidy, no-one is accusing you, and I'm sure this is a big misunderstanding. But there are further developments that would be better discussed down at the station."

You bet it's a misunderstanding. "What sort of developments?" Cassidy asked. The knots in her stomach had quadrupled, tethering her insides together.

Anderson sighed, his lips thinning. "We can do this the—" His words were halted by Robert's guttural, exaggerated cough.

"I think what Detective Anderson means is, if you accompany us to the station, we can sort this out promptly. What do you say?" Robert's eyes pleaded with her for co-operation.

Cassidy squeezed Clair's icy hand. "Why not, I have nothing to hide."

Clair's jaw dropped in protest. "But…"

She wavered before turning her hesitant gaze toward Clair. "I'll be fine. I'm sure I won't be long since I had nothing to do with Christina's death."

Chapter Three

CASSIDY SAT STILL for a few moments, her heart pounding. *Why me?* This is the first time she'd ever been inside an interrogation room and it sent shivers through her body. Her stomach revolted at the stale, lingering scent of cigarettes and alcohol. She found herself wondering what sad soul had sat in the chair before her.

"Why would anyone think I would kill Christina Jacobs?" she asked under her breath.

Detective Anderson's deep voice rang out from behind. She gasped, startled by his sudden presence. "That's a very good question. And one I hope you will be able to answer."

The tension in his words screamed guilty. "But I didn't kill her," Cassidy said with conviction.

He took a seat opposite her and flipped open his notepad. "In the early hours of this morning, we had a report of a break-in at Mr and Mrs Jacobs' retreat. Upon investigation, we discovered it had been ransacked and the body of Christina Jacobs was wrapped in the material you selected for curtains."

Cassidy's pulse sped and she raised an eyebrow in question. "My material?"

His darkened eyes glared up from his notebook. "Yes, your material. We also found this note." He slid an evidence bag across the table.

YOU OWE ME!

Her eyes widened. "I didn't write that note. It doesn't even look like my handwriting."

The sound of his forced laugh sent icy shivers up her spine. "I think we both know that Christina owed you money. In fact, half of Ashton Point heard it, thanks to your public argument yesterday morning in the Tea 4 Two Café."

"Yes, but that was just an argument. Things were said in the heat of the moment. She took me by surprise. After all, my clients were her parents, not Christina." Cassidy folded her arms across her chest and squeezed her fists tight. "I'm sure most people in the café were just as shocked as I was to see her walk through the door."

"Be that as it may, you can't deny that you own a scarf exactly like the one we found wrapped around her neck."

Annoyance at his accusatory attitude started to bubble in her belly. "I won't deny it. I do own a scarf just like it."

"We have a witness that identified you exiting The Classic Curl two days ago wearing this scarf. Is that correct?" he asked, pursing his lips together waiting for her response.

Is it? She racked her brain, so much had happened in the last forty-eight hours. *Two days ago would make it Friday 2nd December.* She vaguely remembered running into Robert Loughlin just after she'd booked a hair appointment with Shelly at The Classic Curl. "You could just say it was Robert, and yes, I ran into him wearing a similar scarf as I came out of the hairdresser. But that still doesn't prove it's mine. Anyone could have ordered it online. Like I said, it's a very popular brand this season."

Cassidy stiffened and she gazed over the table as he jotted down additional notes. From where she was sitting, it looked bad, very bad. Her calm demeanour was starting to crack. Her nerves began to fray at the seams. "After I ran into Robert, I went straight to the Jacobs' retreat to continue working." She paused a moment. "Come to think of it, I didn't have my scarf when I got home. I left it there, which puts a hole straight in the middle of your investigation."

Taken aback by her words, he frowned and glared at her. "How so?"

"Well, if, as you say, you had a call about a break-in and I left my scarf there, anyone could have used it to murder Christina. You find the people who broke in and you find your murderer. All I know is it wasn't me."

He is unbelievable, she thought as she watched his hand scribble more notes. He sat there, practically ignoring her. She never remembered him being this arrogant before.

Cassidy stood and the searing numbness in her legs was a shock to her system. Gripping the edge of the table for support, she said, "I have been very patient, Detective, and I have answered all your questions. So, if there will be nothing else, I'd like to be on my way."

She froze as his sturdy gaze held her to the spot. "For now," he said as he stood, his scraping chair sending shivers up her spine. "But don't leave town."

As if you'd let me. "I wouldn't dream of it. I'm sure you'll be in touch," she said storming from the interrogation room, the jarring movement diffusing the numbness in her legs with every step.

"I can't believe this is happening again," Charlotte said as she paced the foyer of the police station. "I wish I had been there when Detective

Anderson rocked up. I would have happily told him what he could do with his accusations against Cassidy."

Clair huffed. "Great, then I would have been here alone. Waiting for Cassidy, who is being questioned for murder and *you*, for unruly behaviour toward a police officer."

Charlotte pursed her lips and glared at Clair. "Don't be silly, I would never let that happen. But it's like there's some sort of curse on us. Every time something happens in this town, blame it on the McCorrson girls. As if everyone else in this town is innocent."

Clair sat, irritated by Detective Anderson's assuming attitude. "I, for one, am pretty sick and tired of it. It's not like we have spare time to sit around planning the next murder."

She was due to open CC's Cupcake Haven by the end of the year, which was three weeks away. How was she supposed to do that if she had to worry about keeping her baby sister out of jail?

Clair's train of thought was interrupted and her focus turned toward the noise at the counter. Alison, the receptionist, babbled in her high-pitched voice as she spoke somewhat loudly on the phone.

Charlotte flopped down in the seat next to her. "I guess we just wait for Cassidy and go from there. I'm sure there's a simple explanation."

"I hope you're right." Clair's head was starting to pound. She had way too many errands to run today to be wasting time at the police station. *Distraction, I need a distraction.* "So, when is Liam due back?" she asked.

Charlotte's eyes lit up and a blush flooded her expression at the mention of Liam. "Today. I can't wait to see him. I've missed him so much. I know he's only been gone for five days, but it feels like forever when he goes away for work."

Liam had been a godsend a few months back. He lent a helping hand to clear Charlotte's name and restore CC's Simply Cupcakes' stellar reputation. Clair hadn't expected him to stay in Ashton Point after the wedding, but as fate would have it, he and

Charlotte had fallen in love. She smiled at her sister's dreamy gaze.

Clair's head quickly spun around when the scrape of metal on metal grated on her nerves. Cassidy emerged and Clair's heart sank through the floor at the dismayed expression on her face. Bolting from the chair, she threw her arms around her sister and felt the tension ease from Cassidy's body. "Finally. Thank goodness."

"Are you all right?" Charlotte asked as she joined them in the centre of the foyer.

"Yes. I'm fine," Cassidy said as she pulled back.

A familiar sensation of déjà vu danced up Clair's spine. *Why is it that I always seem to be spending an excessive amount of time at this police station?* "What happened in there?"

"Not a lot," Cassidy said with a sigh. "They think someone murdered her when they broke into Christina's parent's retreat."

Charlotte frowned, folding her arms across her chest. "That's it? Did he say anything else?"

Cassidy's gaze caught Alison's prying eyes looking their way. She leant in and they followed her lead. "I'd rather not discuss it here."

Clair smiled, the knot in her gut telling her she knew exactly how Cassidy felt. "Come, let's get out of here. Charlotte needs to head into the shop anyway. You can tell us what happened when we get there," she said as she headed toward the exit.

Within seconds, she froze. An unwelcoming sense of dread washed over her as she spotted Kenneth, the local delivery boy, drop a pile of papers on the coffee table in the waiting room. "Oh no... The morning paper. Christina's death is sure to make the front page."

"Of course it will. Christina owned the paper and she's been murdered." Charlotte paused, sauntering toward the coffee table. "After getting it so wrong and printing false allegations about you and me, Daniel wouldn't dare print anything about Cassidy before checking first." She held the paper up toward her sisters. "See?"

Cassidy gasped, swaying on her feet. Clair cursed as she held tight to her arm. "Easy, Cassidy." Her heart shattered as the headline flashed like a neon sign.

Charlotte's eyes widened and she turned the paper. "What the... No, no, no this isn't going to happen again. 'Third time's a charm for Ashton Point's own Cupcake Killers.' Christina is no longer controlling *The Chronicle*, so what on earth is Daniel doing printing garbage like this? I thought he was better than that."

"Beats me," Clair said. "Last time I spoke to Daniel, he was adamant it was Christina who liked to bend the facts to sell more papers. Now it looks like he's following in her footsteps."

Charlotte folded the paper and shoved it into her bag. "We'll discuss it at the shop."

Cassidy's fiery insides slowly dissolved as she sipped an icy raspberry lemonade. She stood, leaning against the centre table in the baking room, reading Daniel's article for the hundredth time. "This is the most ridiculous pack of lies I've ever heard. Where did he get this information from, anyway? 'Has Cassidy McCorrson's instinct for murder stemmed from her older sisters' or has she branched out to prove, once and for all, that she is the sister that holds all the cards?'" *How totally absurd. Who does he think we are, a serial killing family?*

"I suppose we'll find out soon enough after the police finish their investigation," Cassidy said, her uncertain fate hanging over her head like a gloomy thunderstorm about to hit at full force.

Charlotte and Clair exchanged worried glances. "Um, I'm not sure that's such a good idea," Clair said.

Her words sprouted concern and Cassidy frowned. "What? Why?"

Charlotte's disgruntled tone filled the baking room. "Detective Anderson couldn't solve a murder if all the clues were laid out for him like a map."

"What Charlotte means is, if it weren't for us doing our own investigating, we'd both be in prison now. Doing time for murders we didn't commit," Clair said, her gaze drilling into Charlotte.

Cassidy's heart sank as Clair's words rang true in her mind. After she'd unexpectedly arrived home, her sisters had shared their close brushes with murder. They'd also shared how if it weren't for their individual investigative efforts, she might have had to visit them on weekends in Silverwater Women's Correctional Centre. "Maybe you're right. The last thing I want is to be the convenient scapegoat and have Christina's murder pinned on me."

Charlotte finished pouring the last of the red velvet mixture into the cupcake trays and popped them in the oven. "Okay, then let's look at this from an outsider's perspective," she said wiping her hands down her apron. "I suppose it does look a tad suspicious that she was found strangled with a scarf similar to yours—most probably *is* yours—then wrapped in material you chose for the curtains."

Cassidy's mind was all over the place, sluggish as if she'd done an all-nighter cramming for a test. "Not to mention the note."

"What note?" Clair and Charlotte uttered in unison.

"You never said anything about a note," Charlotte said, the bowl she'd picked up frozen mid-air.

"Didn't I?" She cringed as Clair stepped forward, her crossed arms matching the scowl on her face.

"No, you didn't. Now spill. What note?"

A muffled sigh escaped Cassidy's lips. "There was a note found next to the body. Scribbled on it were the words, 'you owe me.' Detective Anderson assumed I wrote it after my and Christina's very public argument yesterday."

"I hope you put him straight?" Clair asked.

"I certainly did, but…" She trailed off, her gaze roaming the article once more. She couldn't shake the niggle in the base of her neck. Something wasn't right, but she couldn't put her finger on it. "What I don't understand is why Daniel hasn't mentioned it in this article."

"Maybe he doesn't know," said Clair.

A tense knot formed in Cassidy's chest and she continued. "Or maybe he has something else in mind and is keeping it to himself for the time being. Either way, I'm not letting him unravel everything I've worked so hard to achieve with false information. I think Daniel and I need to have a little chat." She gazed up to her sister's inquisitive stares. "Who's with me?"

"I'm in," Clair said as she grabbed her handbag from the table. "But afterwards, I have to drop you home so I can head over to see the Sweets place to meet a contractor."

"No problem."

"No fair." Charlotte pouted, her bottom lip sticking out like a sore thumb. "I have to get these red velvet cakes iced and decorated before I leave.

They need to be ready for Mrs Griffin to pick up, later this afternoon."

A rush of adrenaline bled through her body. "We'll keep you posted," Cassidy called over her shoulder as they exited.

Chapter Four

DANIEL STOOD AT the back of the Ashton Point Chronicle office, his head jolted upward at the chime of the doorbell. His lips thinned. "Of course, I should have expected a visit for you ladies."

Cassidy's eyes narrowed at Daniel's condescending tone. "Why, Daniel? Why would you write all that stuff about me on the front page, when you know it's not true?"

He shrugged his shoulders. "It's nothing personal, it's just business."

Clair gasped and Cassidy's jaw almost hit the ground. "Nothing personal? It's personal to me," Cassidy said, annoyance running through her words.

Clair glared at him through slitted eyes and Cassidy could feel Clair's anger begin to rise in her voice. "You and I both know this paper has taken great pleasure in printing lies about our family. First Charlotte, then me and now you're targeting Cassidy. Why?"

He looked guilty, as if he'd just been caught climbing through his bedroom window after curfew. "I don't make the rules, I just follow them," Daniel snapped.

But Christina is dead. "Whose rules?" Cassidy asked.

He frowned. "Christina's?"

Frustration twisted her stomach into knots. "Christina's your boss and she's no longer around to call the shots, so whose rules are you following?" Daniel paled and a spark of triumph spurred in her gut. "Do you have something to hide, Daniel?"

He huffed and balked at her question. "Hide? Me? I don't know what you're talking about. Even though she may no longer be here, I'm under contract to the paper. My job is to sell newspapers. So, that's what I'm doing."

Cassidy's gut churned with speculation. "Really? It certainly looks like you're making a lot of assumptions. One could say you're covering for the real murderer. Maybe *you* killed her. What better way to hide the truth than to start rumours with that story you wrote?"

"What?" he asked, recoiling at the accusation. "Why would I do that? I had nothing to do with her murder."

"So, you have an alibi then?" she asked, an eyebrow raised.

His eyes darkened. "I don't need an alibi because I didn't murder anyone, but if you must know I was home. Didn't leave my house until I came to work at my normal time, early this morning, to sort the morning edition." Daniel's smug attitude was beginning to grate on Cassidy's highly-strung nerves. "I was all set for a cover page about this year's Christmas parade in honour of poor Mr Hutson when my sources came up with something better. You," he said glaring at Cassidy.

"Oh, come off it, we all know there's no love lost between you and Christina. Some would say you despised her. Especially when she refused to make you a partner in the paper," Clair snapped.

Daniel's eyes widened. *Now we're getting somewhere.* "For that matter, if you have a contract as you say, surely it would be void now that she's dead."

"I wish," he muttered the words so that they were barely audible. He sighed. "Listen, sure, I took a disliking to Christina and I even thought about killing her sometimes, who hasn't? But I didn't." Daniel said, heading over to the coffee machine tucked away in the corner. "I'm sure the majority of residents in Ashton Point have thought about it once or twice. She wasn't the easiest person to get along with. But before you start accusing me of her murder, why don't you take a good look at some people who really had it in for her?"

Clair frowned. "Like who?"

"Like our beloved mayor for starters." Daniel turned his gaze on Cassidy's blank expression. "Surely your sisters told you about their public display on the dance floor at the Gala Dinner last month?"

Cassidy turned to Clair. "What is he talking about?"

Clair slapped her forehead. "Of course. I'd almost forgotten. I didn't see them, but Charlotte told me about it the next day. She said that it was pretty entertaining. Christina and Mayor Windsor were in a heated discussion that ended with some choice words and her storming from the dance floor."

Cassidy's mind began to swim, with information mingling like a whirlpool. "Why am I only hearing about this now?"

Clair's apologetic gaze softened the blow.

"Choice words? Ha. I'd call it more like a threat," Daniel said with a smirk.

"Threat?" Cassidy asked.

"Yes. I was nearby, dancing with Suzi, and Christina said loud enough for those around to overhear, 'I'll see you in hell' and he said, 'not if I see you first.' Then she stormed off toward the exit, leaving him red-faced for all to gawk at."

Cassidy's jaw dropped. "Seriously?"

Daniel leant against the counter and folded his arms. His arrogant expression added to Cassidy's frustration. "Yep, so before you try and convict me, why not give our trusted mayor a visit?"

"How about you do the same?" Clair snapped.

"Yes, Daniel. It works both ways," Cassidy said, leaning in to hold his stare head on. "From now on, you only print the facts. We'll find them for you and neither of us will be convicted of a murder we didn't commit."

Cassidy's gaze watched his Adam's apple ripple as he swallowed. "Fine."

Satisfaction bled through Cassidy's body as Clair drove back home. "Did you notice Daniel didn't mention anything about the note? I thought for sure he'd use it against me… That is, if he knew about it."

"Well, either he doesn't know or he's keeping it to himself for some reason," Clair said as she turned off the main street. "Either way, I don't trust him and I don't think you should either."

Cassidy shook her head, unease gnawing at the base of her gut. "Oh, I don't. Although I am curious about his under-the-breath comment. Did you hear it?" she asked. Cassidy smiled as she watched the clogs in Clair's mind click over.

"Oh, the one about the contract?" Clair said.

"Yeah. I thought it was strange. It makes me think that he's hiding something. It's as if Christina still has him under her control, even from the grave." Pain shot through Cassidy's head. Her mind was whirling at full speed, trying to decipher what Daniel was insinuating.

"Maybe Suzi knows. I could ask her…in a roundabout way," Clair said, a hesitant grin working its way across her face.

Cassidy's curiosity began to eat at her insides. "Maybe. What I really want to know, though, is what happened between Christina and Mayor Windsor on the dance floor?"

Clair shrugged, keeping her eyes glued to the road ahead. "I've no idea. I was a little pre-occupied that night with trying to prove my innocence."

Guilt forced a knot in the back of Cassidy's throat and a shiver of regret raced across her skin. Extending her stay in New York had been a huge mistake. She should have been here to help Clair. *How could I have been so gullible?*

She'd fallen for the perfect man, who had promised her the world, only to find out he was as selfish and self-centred as they come. If only she'd woken up sooner to her blunder, maybe she would have been in Ashton Point to help Clair when she needed her.

A tightness filled Cassidy's chest as Clair continued. "But whatever it was, it must be pretty big. I've never known Brad to lose his cool in public like that."

"I know, me neither. As mayor, I'm sure the last thing he would want is a public scandal." They sat in silence and Cassidy's mind began to jump from one intriguing conclusion to the next. Deception.

Stealing. Blackmail. *What sort of secret would destroy anyone if it went public? Especially in a small town like Ashton Point.* She thought biting her bottom lip.

An affair! She gasped, catching Clair's attention for a split second.

"What's wrong," Clair asked, concern seeping through her words.

Cassidy shook her head. "Nothing, sorry. I was just thinking. What about an affair?"

Clair frowned. "Who, Daniel and Christina?"

"No, no, no. Brad and Christina," Cassidy said turning to face Clair. "What if they were having an affair? We know Christina has had many affairs, her latest with James Hapworth, what's one more? What if he realised what he was doing was wrong and tried to break it off with her? What if he was hoping that by doing it on the dancefloor, in view of everyone in town, she wouldn't cause a scene, but it backfired? They got into a heated argument and then she threatened him."

Clair huffed. "You sound like you're writing an episode of *Home and Away*. I hardly think Brad would be sleeping with Christina."

"What makes you so sure?" Cassidy asked, in a suspicious tone. "She has been known to use her charm to get what she wants." Clair frowned and Cassidy knew in her gut she'd planted the seed of doubt in her sister's mind. "Well…" Cassidy badgered Clair for an answer. When she didn't get one, she continued, feeling she was on the right track. "You know what this town is like for gossip. Stephanie, over at the Classic Curl, happened to mention the other day that prior to Christina's affair with James Hapworth, she was spotted getting chummy with several men here and over at Watson's Creek."

"Really? I thought Brad would never do that to his wife, but now that I think about it, I haven't seen Sheryl around for a while," Clair said as she drove down their street. "Which is highly unusual, as she used to pop into the shop almost every week to get orange and poppy seed cupcakes for her husband."

The tightness in her chest eased a little and a plan started to form in Cassidy's mind. "Well, there's only going to be one way to find out. We ask the mayor what the fight was about. Maybe, if we're lucky, he'll confess to sleeping with Christina."

"I suppose it couldn't hurt to ask. Either way, we'd be able to eliminate him from the suspect list or give Daniel his next front-page story."

Triumph filled Cassidy's heart and she bubbled with satisfaction at her deductive reasoning skills. She'd have the real murderer wrapped up by sunset.

As Clair pulled into the driveway, her gaze turned toward the front porch and the air suddenly vanished from her lungs in one fell swoop.

No, it can't be.

A tallish man stood on the front porch. His bleach-blond, wavy hair, which hung just below his shoulders was tied back neatly in a ponytail. Even with his back turned, there was no mistaking his broad shoulders, prominent torso and tight backside.

Finn! What on earth are you doing in Ashton Point?

After discovering Todd's philandering ways, she'd high-tailed it back to Australia on the first available plane. She'd left without so much as a goodbye to Finn and now he was here, in the flesh, standing on her porch.

"I wonder who that is." Clair said, one eyebrow raised. "I don't recognise his car."

"His name is Finn Beckett," Cassidy said, swallowing the lump in her throat. "He's a freelance travel reporter. He was staying in the same building as Mum and Dad while on assignment in New York. We became good friends."

Clair's eyes widened. "Really? What's he doing here?"

That's a very good question. As far as she knew, his contract in New York had two months left on it. Her fingers twisted together into a ball at her stomach. Cassidy's heart lurched as he turned, his cobalt-blue eyes locking onto hers. It was like being doused with ice cold water. His steely gaze drilling hers.

Please, please, please, don't be here because of Todd. The last thing she wanted to do was confess to her sisters how naive she'd been falling for the wrong man. She'd never live down the embarrassment.

"Well, let's not keep our guest waiting," Clair said as she jumped out of the car like an excited child on Easter morning. "I, for one, can't wait to hear an update on Mum and Dad and what's been happening in The Big Apple."

Chapter Five

FINN STOOD RIGID, his gaze focused on the familiar red-headed beauty seated in the car, and he didn't mean the driver. He'd waited long enough. Just when he'd thought he was making headway with Cassidy, she ups and leaves New York. It didn't matter how long it took and he wouldn't push her, but he was going to get some answers.

A shiver of excitement danced up his spine as the two ladies headed in his direction. He took in the tall, red-head woman as she approached. An older version of Cassidy, but with stunning emerald eyes as big as jewels. He outstretched his hand. "You must be Clair. Cassidy's talked about you so much I feel like I know you already. Or maybe it's Charlotte?"

Clair eased her hand into his. "Right on your first go. And you are?"

His brow creased. She hadn't told her sisters about him. "Finn. Finn Beckett. Your parents live in the building where I was staying and Cassidy and I became friends." *At least I thought we had.* "It was great to have a fellow Aussie to chat with about home. By the way, your Mum and Dad say hello."

Clair paused and her gaze shot from Finn to Cassidy and back again. "Would you like to come in for coffee and cupcakes?"

His stomach knotted. Cassidy stood there silently, as if she were annoyed by his presence. The knots had worked their way up to his throat and it was like talking around a tennis ball. "I'd hate to impose. I've been visiting friends up in the Coffs Harbour and now I'm on my way back down the coast to Sydney."

Clair stepped past Finn, heading for the door. "In that case, you're probably desperate for a good coffee and we have only the best."

Cassidy stood there, silently staring at him. It was as if the beautiful woman he'd met in New York had vanished and been replaced by a mute. "As long as Cassidy is okay with it? I know I arrived unexpectedly and I probably should have called first, but I wasn't sure I'd be welcome."

Clair frowned.

Cassidy spoke for the first time, her voice as perfect as he remembered it. "Of course, you're welcome. Why would you think anything else?"

Finn shrugged, relief filling his chest. "One day you were there and the next you were gone. You left in such a hurry and you didn't even say goodbye. I figured you must have had a good reason, I just hope it wasn't because of me."

Cassidy's eyes widened and her jaw dropped open.

"I'm sure there's a simple explanation but its way too muggy to discuss it out here on the porch," Clair said, opening the door. "Come in and Cassidy can straighten this whole thing out over coffee and cupcakes."

Cassidy smiled and followed Finn and Clair into the kitchen oblivious to their happy banter. How was she going to wiggle her way out of this one? It's not like she could tell the truth.

Gee, it's a really funny story. I left because even though you tried to warn me about what a dirty scumbag Todd was, I didn't listen. He used me to skyrocket his career and when the truth finally hit home, I was so embarrassed I couldn't face the one person who saw it from the start. Like that is going to work?

"Hazelnut coffee okay with you, Finn? It's my favourite," Clair asked as she busied herself by the Nespresso machine.

Finn's hand shot to his stomach as a hunger growl grumbled from his belly like a muted fog horn. "Sorry about that, guess I was hungrier than I thought. Hazelnut sounds great. Did you mention something about cupcakes?"

A spark of hope filled Cassidy at the mention of Charlotte's cupcakes. Her mind was working overtime, plotting the perfect escape plan. Heading for the fridge, she grabbed the cupcake container and placed it on the table. "We certainly do." She paused before opening the lid. "Charlotte's cupcakes."

The growling of his stomach doubled. "From CC's Simply Cupcakes?"

Both Cassidy and Clair smiled. "One and the same. Charlotte tries to keep the fridge stocked with cupcakes and if she doesn't, we tie her down until she makes some."

A giggle erupted from the direction of the coffee machine. "Don't be silly, Cassidy, we do not tie her down. We lock the doors and steal her keys." A warm bout of laughter filled the kitchen, easing the turmoil in Cassidy's gut.

"I'm sorry, it's just that Cassidy raved about Charlotte's cupcakes the entire time she was in New York and I never thought I'd get to taste them," he said, his eyes glued to the container.

"Well, don't let us stop you. Here," Cassidy said, placing a cupcake on a plate and sliding it in his direction.

Clair placed a steaming coffee in front of him and sat beside Cassidy. Both women watched as he devoured the red velvet treat in seconds.

"That has to be the best cupcake I've ever tasted," Finn said, wiping the corners of his mouth with his ring finger.

Satisfaction bloomed in Cassidy's belly. "Told you so. Now you see why I had to come home?"

Clair raised an eyebrow and glared at her. "Because of Charlotte's cupcakes?"

"Not just the cupcakes. For both of you. I agreed to design the interior of your new shop over at the Sweets mansion, remember? And I couldn't really do that from the other side of the world, could I?" Cassidy's heart raced and she prayed she sounded convincing enough to stop the third-degree. "Besides, Mum was snowed under with work and I'd outstayed my welcome. I could see they were getting restless. It was time to come home."

"So, that meant you couldn't even say goodbye before you left?" Finn said, annoyance etched in his tone.

Clair chimed in. "Yes, Cassidy, did that mean you couldn't say goodbye to Finn?"

Her stomach dropped as she took in Clair's frozen expression. *Oh goodness, she's guessed I'm lying.* "You're right. I'm sorry. I should have told you I was heading back to Australia. It all happened so fast. I managed to get a quick flight home at a great price."

"Speaking of the Sweets mansion." Clair checked the time on her wristwatch. "I need to head over to the property to meet the contractor who will be fixing the back-patio decking." Clair stood and placed her coffee cup in the dishwasher. "Nice to meet you, Finn. If you're not doing anything later, it's pizza night tonight. You're more than welcome to join us. I'm sure Charlotte would love to meet you, and you can fill us in on what's happening with Mum and Dad. And also, the mischief our little sister got up to in New York. Cassidy, while I'm out, why don't you fill Finn in on what's been happening with you over the past few days? Always better to hear it straight from the horse's mouth."

Pizza? Seriously? Cassidy's chest hurt as the walls around seemed to cave in all at once. She forced a smile as Clair grabbed her bag and headed out. "We'll chat later, Cassidy," she said over her shoulder.

Great. Well, "chat later" was short for, "You're hiding something and I'm going to find out what it is if it kills me."

Finn sat back in his chair, his gaze firmly rooted on her. "She's exactly as you described. What did she mean about filling me in on what's been happening over the last few days?"

Oh boy, this could take a while. She sighed and flicked her hand in an upward direction in what she hoped was a nonchalant fashion. "Oh, it's all a big misunderstanding. Nothing for you to worry about."

He frowned. "What is?"

Her stomach churned just thinking about his reaction when she told him of her untimely run-in with the law. *Change the subject.* "I really am sorry for not saying goodbye before I left."

The hurt in his eyes gutted her. "I thought we were friends…good friends," he said.

She felt a warm blush work its way up her neck. "We are."

"Did you leave because of me?" he asked, the uncertainty in his gaze was like a dagger to her heart.

She gasped in shock. "No. Absolutely not."

He continued. "Was it because of Todd?"

"Todd?" Panic scuttled up her spine. "Why would you think that?"

"He came by the day after you left, looking for you," Finn said, taking another sip of his coffee. "He wasn't too happy when I told him you'd gone back to Australia. Started ranting and raving about how you've ruined everything."

I *ruined everything? He breaks my heart and then has the gall to blame me for ruining his life? Ha.*

"Then he accused me of turning you against him, of interfering in your relationship." Finn's words rang out across the kitchen like alarm bells. "He insinuated that we were more than friends and that's why you left. So you didn't have to make a choice between us. I'd even go as far as saying he warned me to stay away from you."

Cassidy's jaw dropped. Rage seethed in her belly like a bubbling cauldron. "The nerve of that man. I don't know what I ever saw in him." Her brain was about to explode with the ways she'd like to make Todd pay, but doing so wouldn't change the outcome. Finn's sweet voice broke through her hardened thoughts.

"What did he do, Cassidy? Is he why you left so suddenly?" Finn asked.

Yes, but please don't make me relive the embarrassment. "It doesn't matter now. I can't turn back time. More to the point I don't want to. All I can do is apologise and promise it will never happen again. Can you live with that?"

Finn sat still, as if contemplating her words. A smile turned up the corner of his lips. "Yeah, I can live with that, as long as you promise to never leave without saying goodbye again."

She smiled and contentment filled her heart. "Promise."

"So, what was your sister talking about?" Finn asked.

"Okay, you win. I guess you'll find out sooner or later. Seems the police think I may have murdered someone," she said in a casual tone hoping to bypass the interrogation.

Finn paled and shot to his feet. "What?"

Cassidy stood, her heart racing like a greyhound on the home stretch. The rich, woody scent of his aftershave filled her nostrils and she paused. The aroma reminded her of all the good times they'd spent together. *Focus.* "I told you, it's a big misunderstanding."

"How can accusing you of murder be a misunderstanding?" He folded his arms across his chest like a bouncer and drilled his eyes into her soul. "Tell me the whole story, and don't leave a single detail out."

Cassidy's heart skipped a beat. "I'm sure the real murderer will be caught any day now." *If I have my way, they will.* "There's no real need to rehash the story all over again." Her heart jumped into her throat and her stomach clenched at his expression of determination.

"I've nowhere to be, so I can stand here all day. I'm happy to wait as long as I need to, to get the truth," Finn said with a shrug. "Or?"

"Or what?" she asked.

"Or, I'm sure I can dredge up some interesting stories to tell your sisters about your wild escapades in New York," he said with a smirk.

Cassidy thrust her hands on her hips. "You wouldn't dare."

A sneer edged the corner of his mouth. "Isn't that what friends are for?"

She threw her arms up in resignation, her body revelling in the playful banter. "Okay, okay, but it might take a while." He stood in silence and simply glared at her, waiting. She rolled her eyes and sighed heading toward the TV room. "All right, follow me."

Chapter Six

"WAIT A MINUTE," Finn said rubbing his chin in thought. "Let me get this right. They found a scarf like yours, tied around this Christina woman's throat, and she was wrapped in the material you chose for the curtains in her parent's retreat. And they think you killed her just because you have the same scarf?"

Cassidy nodded and tucked her foot underneath her on the couch. She hadn't realised how much she'd missed Finn until she'd seen him standing on the porch. A twinge of regret flooded her chest. He had quickly become her best friend. "That, the note, and the open argument we had in the Tea 4 Two Café. Sounds crazy right?"

"Sounds like the plot of some fictional movie, if you ask me. It's obvious someone is trying to frame you." Finn said, turning to face Cassidy square on.

A tremor leaped up her spine as she lost herself a moment in the depths of his cobalt-blue eyes. He slid his hands around hers and her tremors eased at his touch.

"You, Cassidy McCorrson are the most genuine, wonderful, caring woman I know. You shouldn't have to face this alone."

She swallowed the lump in her throat as his beautiful words washed over her. "I…I'm not really alone. I have my sisters."

"Yes, you do, and I can help," he said, sincerity etched in his tone.

Cassidy felt her cheeks redden. "What do you mean?"

"Friends help friends out when they're in need. I finished my contract in New York early so I'm between jobs at the moment. If you'll let me, I'd like to stick around town until I know you're safe and not stuck in a jail cell somewhere for a crime you didn't commit. What do you say? Would that be all right with you?" he asked.

Butterflies danced a feast in her stomach. The thought of spending more time with Finn was a welcomed relief. She'd been a fool not to trust him in New York, and she'd be a fool to throw away her chance now. She smiled. "Sure. That would be fine with me."

"Hello… Cassidy, are you home?" A strong male voice bellowed from the front of the house.

Finn's back straightened and his gaze shot toward the entrance. "Who's that?"

"Sounds like Mason, Clair's boyfriend." Cassidy glanced at her watch. "Holy cow, it's almost four-thirty. Where did that time go?"

Finn relaxed back on the lounge and chuckled. "Between me updating you on my adventures and you explaining the whole murder situation, seems time got away from us."

"There you are," Mason said as he sauntered in, his eyes quickly homing in on the additional male in the room. "You must be Finn. Clair mentioned she'd met you this afternoon. I'm Mason Hapworth," he said as they shook hands.

"Finn Beckett, nice to meet you," he said as he stood eye to eye with Mason. Cassidy looked at the two robust men standing before her and the room suddenly felt overpowered with testosterone. "Where's Clair?" she asked.

Clair's voice called from the kitchen. "In here… Anyone for pizza?"

"Sounds like my kind of meal," Finn said with a smile that gave her heart a flutter.

As they converged on Clair in the kitchen, Mason and Finn were already deep in conversation behind her. "What time will Charlotte be home?" Cassidy asked.

Clair threw her wavy red locks over her shoulder and narrowed her eyes at Cassidy. "She won't."

"What do you mean she won't? I thought Liam was back today?"

"He is. Seems he'll be treating her to a superb five-star dinner at the new Vietnamese restaurant, The Wonders of Saigon," Clair said as she busily packed away some groceries. "I've heard amazing reports about the food. Some say it's the best they've ever tasted. Guess it will just be us four for pizza."

"Better odds for me," Finn said with a cheeky smirk. "Two less to interrogate me on your sister's antics in New York."

Antics… Oh no, what if he spills the beans about Todd? Cassidy's eyes widened and her pulse raced. Clair would never forgive her if she found out about her blunder with Todd from a total stranger.

"We have some time before dinner, so why don't you guys go and get acquainted? Cassidy and I'll order the pizzas and finish putting the groceries away," Clair said, her gaze frozen on her man.

Mason sidled up to Clair and planted a peck on her cheek. "I can take a hint. Come on, Finn, seems they need some girl time. We'll be out back if you need us."

Finn's gaze held Cassidy stationary, a silent plea for her confirmation. Cassidy smiled. "I'm sure Mason is eager to begin the interrogation, but promise me you won't say anything 'til I can defend myself?"

Cassidy's heart skipped a beat as Finn play-punched her in the shoulder. "Promise," he said. Heat rose from her belly as her gaze stuck to his tight derriere until it vanished.

"Oh, boy, I know that look," Clair's voice broke through Cassidy's trance.

"What on earth are you talking about?" Cassidy asked, frowning at her nosy sister.

Clair folded her arms across her chest. "You like Finn, and I don't mean as a friend."

Cassidy froze and she felt the blood drain from her face. *Do I?*

Clair grabbed Cassidy's arm and pulled her into the closest chair. "We can worry about your feelings for Finn later. You've never opened up about why you arrived home early from New York and judging by Finn's sudden appearance on our doorstep, I'm guessing he doesn't know the answer either. Spill."

She was still processing the unexpected emotions that echoed through her mind. Cassidy's body remembered the electric buzz that ran through it when she'd known she and Finn were going to spend time together. She always thought it was because their friendship had grown closer. Could she have had deeper feelings for Finn and not known it?

Clair's voice finally registered. "Sorry, what did you say?"

"Why did you come back early?" Clair asked again.

Cassidy pushed thoughts of Finn to the back of her mind. Time to face the music. She sighed and dove in head first. "Because I got my heart broken and I wanted to get as far away as possible from the man who did it."

Clair's eyebrows rose. "By Finn?"

Her chest tightened at Clair's assumption. "Gosh no. Finn is like my best friend. I met this guy called Todd Williams. I was too naive to see him for what he really was. A cheating scumbag. He worked on Wall Street in one of the top companies in New York. He was the most amazing man I'd ever met, or so I thought. I fell hard and fast. But it turned out it was all fake. He'd do anything to climb the corporate ladder, including me. Thank goodness he showed his true colours before it went that far. I really don't want to rehash it all again, but when I found out what a fool I'd been, I had to get out of there. It was suffocating. Finn tried to warn me, but I didn't listen. I was embarrassed and I knew he'd think I was a gullible jerk for not listening to him. All I could think about was getting home as soon as I could. I know it was rude of me and I should have said goodbye."

"Does Finn know what happened with Todd?" Clair asked.

Cassidy shook her head. "No, not the whole story. He saw through Todd's bogus personality right from the start."

"Why didn't you tell us before now?" Clair asked, her eyes glazing over with moisture. "You have to know we'd be here for you."

Deep down in the depths of her gut, Cassidy knew her sisters would never let her down, but her insecurities had kept her from confessing. "I know. I guess I was just embarrassed. I'd made some silly decisions when it came to Todd and I had to come to terms with them before I could move forward."

"I see. Do I need to arrange to have his kneecaps broken?" Clair asked in her best Italian Mafia voice. Love for her sister bloomed in her heart and they both burst out laughing. "No, he's not worth it, but promise me you'll let me tell Finn in my own time." Clair smiled and nodded. "Besides, I have bigger fish to fry, namely trying to prove I didn't strangle Christina with my scarf."

It had been a huge relief to finally come clean about Todd. It was as if a tonne of bricks had been lifted off her heart. Since the pizza had arrived, Clair's earlier words had played on repeat in her mind.

You like Finn, and I don't mean as a friend... You have feelings for Finn.

Finn was her best friend, not her boyfriend. She doubted he even looked at her that way. The thought chased any notion of a future together from her mind. Her focus was on proving her innocence and getting her career back on track. Men could wait.

By the time they'd finished the pizza, it felt like old times. She was comfortable in Finn's presence. Just as if they were back in her parent's apartment watching one of his adventure movies. Carb overload. "I cannot believe I ate a whole pizza. I feel like my stomach is about to burst," Cassidy said, holding her belly.

Finn chuckled and glanced from Cassidy to Clair and back again. "Best pizza I've had in a long time. But I seem to remember a red-head who thought she could eat more pizza than me. She even challenged me to a pizza eating contest."

Cassidy's jaw dropped and nausea welled in the pit of her stomach. "Oh no, please don't talk about that."

Clair's eyes lit up like a firecracker. "Oh, do tell. This should be good."

Cassidy pointed at Finn and glared daggers in his direction. "Don't you dare, mister, or I'll tell them about the time you were caught with your pants down in the middle of Madison Square Garden." Finn paled and she knew she'd won. The room erupted into laughter. Her belly ached, but she wasn't sure if it was from laughing so hard or the copious amounts of pizza she'd ingested.

Cassidy jumped as the unexpected shrill of the doorbell filled the house. "Who could that be?" Clair asked, wiping a tear from her eye. "I don't suppose Charlotte has misplaced her key?"

"Goodness knows. I'll get it," Cassidy said as she dragged her carb-laden body toward the front door. She expected to see the smiling face of Charlotte, but she froze when she saw who it was.

Detective Anderson stood at the door with Robert to his right and Kayne to his left. Judging by his folded arms and the stern look on their faces it wasn't a social call. "Can I help you, Detective?" She could almost hear her heart beating right out of her chest.

Cassidy felt her stomach curdle as he handed her a piece of paper. "Cassidy, just the person I was looking for. I have a search warrant here to search the inside of your house for evidence."

"Evidence?" Cassidy's mouth went dry as she scanned the paper in her shaky hands.

"Who is it," Clair asked as she headed down the hall toward the door. Clair stopped suddenly as Detective Anderson took a step inside the house. "What are you doing here?"

"As I've explained to Cassidy, we have a search warrant for the interior of your house and the sooner we get it done, the sooner we can leave," Anderson snapped. "Now, if you would kindly show us the way, Robert and I'll start with the bedrooms and en-suites, Kayne you take the living areas and we'll work our way back to the kitchen area."

Cassidy's head spun like an out of control spinning top. Her legs were like lead weights stuck at the bottom of the ocean. "You can't honestly think I had anything to do with Christina's murder."

"We'll know soon enough," he said barrelling toward the kitchen, Robert and Kayne close on his heels.

Cassidy's brain finally sent the message for her feet to move double time to keep pace with him. They were met in the kitchen by two annoyed men in need of an explanation. "Finn, this is Detective Anderson, Robert and Kayne from the Ashton Point police department. They have a search warrant."

"What?" Finn said, taking a protective step toward Cassidy.

Robert held up his hands for calm. "Listen, we're just doing our jobs and following procedure."

Cassidy rolled her shoulders back and sucked in a lungful of air. "I have nothing to hide, so this should be the shortest search in history. Follow me." Cassidy held her head high and guided Robert and Detective Anderson toward the bedrooms, her hands clenched at her sides so hard she thought she'd draw blood.

Kayne stepped in front of her and held his hand across the doorway, blocking entry to her room. "Thank you. If you would kindly wait with the others in the kitchen, we'll let you know when we're done."

Cassidy moved in auto-pilot, her body numb, a trickle of sweat beaded her forehead. Walking back into the kitchen was like walking into a championship boxing fight, all eyes glued to her, waiting for her next move.

"What's going on?" Clair asked as her arms encased her sister. "I can't believe this is happening."

Cassidy cringed as Clair's icy arms met with her numb exterior. "Believe it. They said to wait here with you until they finished." Cassidy's mind was so busy running over her movements over the past week that she hadn't noticed Finn move up beside her and take Clair's position.

"Did they say anything else?" Finn asked, in a soothing tone.

Cassidy's nerves were beginning to fray. "No, they just said wait here. Please tell me I'm going to wake up and this is all a dream?"

"But if it were a dream then I wouldn't be here," Finn said as he brushed a stray curl behind Cassidy's ear, his mesmerising eyes never leaving hers. "And I hope you're happy I'm here."

In the midst of chaos, the one calming factor was Finn. "I am."

Cassidy's thoughts were interrupted by a prickly sensation running through her body, as if someone had just walked over her grave. She spun and her body froze, her gaze locked on the plastic bag full of hundred-dollar notes in Robert's hand. Anderson moved up beside him.

"Care to explain, Cassidy?" he asked.

She gasped. "That's not mine." Her chest tightened and she felt the air drain from her lungs. She turned to Clair, her eyes begging for her trust. "Clair, I've never seen that bag of money before."

Her life was crumbling around her ears and she was helpless to do anything about it.

Kayne piped up. "It was found underneath your mattress."

"Mmmm. Not a very original position, if you ask me." Robert held up the bag toward Anderson. "I'd say it looks like around $17,500, wouldn't you?"

"I told you, it's not mine." Cassidy's insides felt like a tight ball of frustration ready to detonate.

"Then how do you explain it in your room?" Anderson asked.

No, no, no this isn't happening. Silence filled the room. All eyes turned on her and her stomach revolted at the inquisition. "I can't. I don't know how it got in my room. I didn't put it there and if I didn't, someone else must have." Cassidy's heart lurched into her throat and panic flooded her chest. Kayne stepped toward her and the next words out of his mouth chilled her to the core.

"Cassidy McCorrson… You're under arrest for the murder of Christina Jacobs."

Chapter Seven

CLAIR'S HEART SANK at the look of panic on Cassidy's face as Kayne pulled out a pair of handcuffs. "You can't be serious...You're going to cuff her?" Clair said, her voice three octaves higher than normal.

"This is crazy," Mason said shaking his head. "She wouldn't hurt a fly."

Cassidy took a step backwards toward Finn. "I've already told you, that money is not mine."

Detective Anderson grunted and an irritated sigh escaped his lips. "We found the money in your room. Combined with the information we already have and the argument yesterday morning where half the town heard you threaten Christina Jacobs, it's enough to make an arrest."

"That was something I said in the heat of the moment," Cassidy said, her eyes shooting from one person to another. "I didn't mean it."

"Of course, you didn't," Finn said frowning, his body stiff.

"Close enough for me," Detective Anderson said. "Let's go."

Clair watched helplessly as Kayne cuffed her sister and led her out to the police car, Anderson and Robert shuffling behind. Clair marched out after them, two riled men hot on her tail. "Are you really going to try and pin this murder on my sister?"

"The evidence doesn't lie," Anderson barked.

"Oh, really." Clair stood on the front steps, glaring at the scene before her, rage bellowing inside her chest. "Would that be the same sort of evidence that convinced you I was cursed and a murderer?"

Anderson's eyes narrowed and he took a calculated step toward Clair. "This is different. Now, if you have any hope of saving your sister, I suggest you get her a good lawyer," he said as he turned and got into the driver's seat.

"Hang tight, Cassidy, we'll be down as soon as we can to get you out." They drove away and Clair's heart exploded in her chest as she saw Cassidy's head turn and look out the back window, her eyes moist with tears.

"I can't believe this," Finn said pacing the front porch. "We have to do something. We can't leave her in jail."

Clair spun and looked at them, her insides seething like hot lava. "She's not going to stay in jail for long, Caroline will help us out." Clair paused a moment. "Oh dear, that's if she's back in town. I know she went travelling after her Stuart passed away. If she's not back, our last resort is to ring Dad, it's not like he'll be able to do much from New York. He'll be able to make some calls and point us in the right direction. Anderson's gotten it wrong before and he's gotten it wrong now. But we have to play it smart. There's only one way to stop the accusations against Cassidy... We have to find the real murderer."

Finn stepped up to Clair. "Count me in for however long it takes."

"Me too," Mason added. "Who's Caroline?"

"She's a lawyer who used to work with my dad in his practice here in Ashton Point. They've been best friends since forever. She retired and was caring for her ill husband before he passed, but she always said if we need anything to call, and we definitely need her help." Clair rushed back inside and gathered her bag and keys.

"What can I do?" Finn asked.

"You could head to the station. If I know Cassidy, she'll be freaking out."

Finn nodded and grabbed his keys and wallet from his bag.

Clair continued. "Mason and I will head over to Caroline's and explain the situation. We'll meet you there. I'll call Charlotte and get her and Liam to drop in and see Daniel on the way, to make sure Cassidy's arrest isn't front page news."

Clair wanted to scream at the top of her lungs, but it wouldn't get Cassidy out any sooner.

How is it murder is always attracted to us like a bee is to honey?

Finn pushed through the glass doors of the police station, a cool gust of air hitting him square in the face. His heart pounded inside his chest. He couldn't fathom what Cassidy must be going through right now. Frightened, alone, and scared out of her mind.

Finn approached the counter and was greeted by a youngish, petite woman sporting strawberry-coloured glasses. "Excuse me. I'd like to see Cassidy McCorrson please."

Her eyebrows rose. "And you are?"

He paused a moment sucking in a deep breath, his adrenaline levels rising by the second. "Finn Beckett."

"I'm sorry, Finn, but Cassidy is unable to have visitors."

Finn's chest felt like it was ready to shatter. His gaze caught the lady's name badge. "Alison, I'm sure you can imagine how upset and scared Cassidy must be feeling right now. I know it's not normal to have visitors, but do you think you could make an exception this once?" He flashed a suave smile in her direction and her cheeks turned the same red as her glasses.

"Take a seat and I'll see what I can do," she said, gifting him a huge smile.

Unable to sit, Finn paced the foyer. With each minute that passed, his anxiety increased. He felt like he was back in the hustle and bustle of chaotic New York, where crime was a common occurrence he'd seen way too much of.

"Excuse me, Mr Beckett. I'm afraid the answer is no. You'll have to wait 'til her family and lawyer get here and discuss it with them," Alison said from her perch behind the counter.

Family? The words gripped his heart like a vice. His mouth kicked in before his mind caught up. "I'm kind of family. Cassidy is my girlfriend. We started dating when she was visiting her parents in New York."

Alison's jaw just about hit the counter. "Boyfriend?" She looked him up and down. "Lucky Cassidy, but I'm afraid the answer is still no."

Clair's blood boiled as she stood off to the side of the counter while Caroline worked her magic on Detective Anderson. Caroline's hands moved double time, gesturing in all directions as the conversation became animated. When her dad first opened his law practice in town, Caroline had been like an aunt to them. He always said, if it weren't for Caroline coming on board as his partner, he would never have enjoyed being a lawyer as much as he did. She had a heart as big as Far Lap and considering she was a 5-foot-tall ball of energy with silver-streaked hair, people didn't mess with her very often.

Alison sat behind the reception desk and stared at Clair over her prissy little red glasses. Clair hadn't been this annoyed since they'd tried to accuse her of murder. *Even after living in Ashton Point for three years, the people in this town don't know us very well, if they think we would murder someone in cold blood.*

"Do you want to find out if we can see Cassidy?" Liam asked, his deep voice breaking her line of thought.

Clair shook her head, her jumpy fingers tapped against her leg. "No, I want to be here, in case Caroline needs me for anything." She glanced over toward the entrance and she rubbed her temple, trying to alleviate the growing pain. "Come on, Charlotte. How long does it take to read the riot act to Daniel?" Fed up with standing, she took a seat next to Mason and he eased his hand over hers.

"I'm sure Charlotte will be here as soon as she is done," Mason said.

No sooner had he spoken the words, the glass entry doors flew open and Charlotte entered as if a winter storm had just descended on Ashton Point Police station. Liam's protective embrace held her solidly to his side.

"Charlotte, thank goodness," she said bolting off the chair and into her sister's arms. Mason and Finn stood beside them. Charlotte's eyes shot to Caroline, who was still at the counter deep in conversation. "What is going on?"

"I wish I knew. Caroline asked us to wait here while she sussed out the situation," Clair said, her stomach ready to bring up the pizza she'd eaten earlier. "How did you go with Daniel?"

"Piece of cake," Charlotte said flicking her hand casually.

"How you holding up, Clair?" Liam asked.

She sucked in a deep breath. It was as if her whole body were a single strand of hair about to snap under the pressure. "It isn't about me right now, it's about Cassidy and proving they have the wrong person."

"I can't believe this is happening. How on earth did that money end up in Cassidy's room?" Charlotte said easing back into Liam's arm.

Clair shrugged. "I have no idea and I bet CC's Simply Cupcakes that Cassidy has no idea either. The only answer that seems logical is someone planted it. And whoever is the culprit is doing a bang-up job of setting Cassidy up to take the fall."

Caroline's sharp voice grabbed their attention. "Very well, Detective Anderson. Let me converse with my clients." She spun on her heel and stormed toward them. "Charlotte, thank you for coming. Liam, good to see you," she said, nodding toward them.

A strained smile spread across Liam's face as he acknowledged her greeting with a nod.

"Of course, I wouldn't be anywhere else. Can you tell us what's going on?" Charlotte asked in a nervous tone.

Caroline flicked her fringe from her eyes. "It doesn't look good, I'm afraid, but I've seen worse cases than this, so I don't want you to worry. I will not let Cassidy pay for a crime she didn't commit."

Clair felt the blood drain from her face as she caught Charlotte's shocked expression. *Neither will I.* "You said something about conversing with your clients?"

"Yes, seems that man is determined to pin this crime on Cassidy." Audible gasps from all five echoed through the station foyer. Caroline paused and pursed her lips, holding up her hand. "Now, now. Don't panic. He's just trying to throw his weight around, but he doesn't know who he's up against. As soon as we have the full story, we can work out a plan of action."

Charlotte frowned. "The full story?"

"Yes, he's bringing Cassidy around now and I'll be in there with her the whole time. Rest assured, I will not let her be bullied. You all will have to wait out here, I'm afraid," Caroline said shaking her head. "I swear, that man just likes to hear the sound of his own voice."

"We'll be right here when you come out," Mason said, smiling in Clair's direction.

Relief surged through Clair's body. "Thank you, Caroline. We owe you big time."

"Nonsense," she said, her golden-brown eyes glowing with love. "You girls are like family, it's the least I can do. Detective Anderson is bringing Cassidy in as we speak."

Chapter Eight

CASSIDY SAT IN the interview room, next to Caroline. Her stomach was about to do a double flip from all the built-up tension in the room.

"Detective, now that I have had a chance to speak to my client, how about you fill us in on this so-called evidence you have acquired?" Caroline placed her clasped hands on the table in front of her.

Detective Anderson pulled out his chair and sat, his frown forming a familiar monobrow. "Very well. As you have probably heard, we found Christina Jacobs body yesterday morning."

Caroline nodded. "Yes, Detective, I'm well aware of that fact."

"Christina's next of kin have been informed and we've contacted her lawyer. I'm aware from the conversation in the café between your client and the deceased that he was due in Ashton Point at the end of the week. His services will obviously no longer be needed. The body was found in her parent's retreat, wrapped in curtain material chosen by your client, and strangled with Cassidy McCorrson's scarf."

"Or one similar," Cassidy said, unable to keep the anger from her tone. "I told you I left mine behind in the Jacobs' house the other day. And don't forget the break-in."

Caroline's eyes widened. "What break-in?"

He continued. "We got a tip of a break-in at the Jacobs' place. On arrival, we found Christina's body and a note that said, 'you owe me.'"

"If my client did, in fact, leave her scarf at the location as indicated, anyone could have broken in and used it, implicating an innocent woman. They also could have written that note. Was anything taken in the break-in?"

"The place had been ransacked. At present, we are still investigating." Anderson forged ahead. "And a large sum of money was discovered in Cassidy's bedroom at her place of residence."

Cassidy saw red. "I told you, that money is not mine. It must have been planted." Caroline placed a calming hand on Cassidy's forearm and made a shushing shape with her lips.

"As my client has just stated, she has no knowledge of this so-called money. As far as I can see, you're grasping at straws, Detective Anderson. Do you have irrefutable evidence that the scarf or the money belongs to my client?" Caroline asked. "Such as fingerprints, maybe?"

He frowned. "We're still waiting on the results."

Caroline smirked and a sliver of relief skittled up Cassidy's spine. "That would be a no then, Detective?" He grunted. "What else do you have?"

He continued. "There was the public argument between Cassidy and the victim where she threatened to get her money one way or another. The scarf was tied with a very distinctive knot, a knot used in sailing. A bowline knot, I think it's called."

Cassidy's blood froze as she glanced toward Caroline. *Oh no, why that knot?* She knew it well. It was a favourite of their father's. They used to sail a lot when they were younger and it was one of the knots their dad had taught them.

"What's so special about a bowline knot?" Caroline asked.

Detective Anderson cleared his throat, his gaze drilling into Caroline as if no-one else were in the room. "It's special because it's a loop knot allowing the end to be threaded through the loop, thus making a noose or a weapon. It can be tied easily with one hand, for instance, if someone were holding another down with one hand, they could easily tie the knot with the other. It's often known as King of the Knots and works extremely well under load. And would someone who has owned various types of sailing vessels over the years be privy to this information?"

"Really, Detective. Does my client look like a person who could hold down a struggling body with one hand, while tying a knot with the other? If that's all you have to go on? It's flimsy at best, not to mention circumstantial," Caroline said calmly but the twitch in her jaw let Anderson know she was anything but. "We live on the central coast of New South Wales. Most people in Ashton Point own a boat. I own a boat and I know how to tie a bowline knot. Does that mean I'm a murderer as well? What about you Detective? Do you own a boat?"

"No," he snapped.

"Why is that, Detective? Do you not like the ocean?" Caroline asked smugly. It was like a sparring match between two archenemies.

"Although it's none of your business, when I was around eight years old, I was stung by a box jellyfish in north Queensland while on holiday with my family. It nearly killed me and I haven't been able to go back out on the ocean since," he said.

"Yet you work in a coastal town, where boating is the number one tourist attraction. How interesting," Cassidy said under her breath.

His glare darkened. "Doesn't mean I have to go out on the water. That's what the water police are for." His gaze turned back to Cassidy. "Do you know a woman by the name of Agnus Willowbrook, Miss McCorrson?"

The name Agnus Willowbrook brought back wonderful memories of a lovely lady. One that reminded her of her own grandmother. Cassidy had redesigned the interior of her home to cater to her wheelchair. "Yes, I know Agnus Willowbrook. I worked on her house about six months ago."

"She passed away about two months ago."

Cassidy's heart clenched and her hand flew to her chest. "Oh no, that poor woman."

"If we look into your past clients, how many more bodies do you think we'll find?" he asked, his tone menacing.

Her jaw dropped open. "None."

"Detective, if you are going to arrest my client for this woman's death, please do. And by my calculations, your time is up for holding Cassidy in relation to Miss Jacob's murder."

He squeezed the bridge of his nose. "No, Ms Tuscon, I am not arresting Cassidy in association to Mrs Willowbrook's death, at least not yet, but I will be looking into it further."

"What about Miss Jacob's murder?" Caroline asked.

"Although it's against my better judgement, Cassidy is free to go at this time. I won't be charging her just yet." His gaze turned on Cassidy. "But don't leave town. And it might be an idea to let your lawyer know your whereabouts."

What am I, a child? Fury burned in her veins. Cassidy wanted to tell him exactly what he could do with his proviso.

"Well, it's about time," Caroline said smugly as she stood. "And if you have any further questions for my client, please direct them to me." She trotted from the room, Cassidy in tow.

Caroline's flowy silver hair swished back and forth across her shoulders as they walked out to meet the others. "That man is the most irritating person I know."

"What happened?" Finn asked as they all converged on them when they exited.

Cassidy's heart melted just a little at the concern etched in his gaze. "Caroline was amazing. She handled him like he was putty in her hands."

A crimson blush worked its way across Caroline's cheeks and she brushed the comment aside with a casual swish of her hand.

"Don't be so blasé about it, Caroline, if it weren't for you, I'd be charged with murder right now and back in that cell. And I can tell you, that is a place I do not want to revisit."

"Not an option, young lady. I will not let that happen." Caroline gave each woman a hug. "Gentlemen, take these women home. I think they've had enough excitement for one night. I'll get to work but call me if you need anything or if Detective Anderson makes another unscheduled visit."

Exhaustion hit Cassidy and it was as if she'd suddenly been dumped by a ten-foot wave. "Home sounds good to me."

"Definitely," Charlotte said, threading her arm around Liam. "Do you need a lift or will you ride back with Finn?"

All eyes turned to Cassidy, waiting for her answer. *Why wouldn't I go back with Finn? After all, he is a good friend.* "Yes, as long as it's all right with Finn."

Finn smiled. "Of course. It will give us a little more time to chat."

Her stomach coiled. She knew exactly what he wanted to chat about. Todd.

"Okay, see you at home," Clair said turning to Mason. "Shall we?" he nodded and they followed Charlotte and Liam out.

"What a day, possibly one of the worst days of my life." Cassidy sighed, closing her eyes and leaning her head back on the seat.

"Worse than what happened with Todd?" he asked.

Cassidy's eyes opened and her head snapped up. "What has Todd got to do with any of this?"

"Well, it wasn't hard to work out that you left because of him. One day you were madly in love, preparing to spend a white Christmas with the love of your life, and the next you were gone. I just don't know why or if I need to beat him to a pulp...again, for hurting you."

Cassidy's brow creased. "Again. What do you mean, again? What did you do?" His lips tightened and Cassidy felt the tension between them skyrocket. "Finn... What happened after I left New York? You said Todd came around and blamed me for ruining his life."

Finn nodded. "Yes, he did. The first time he came to find you."

"First?" she said as she pulled back, her shoulder butting up against the window.

"He came back again the next day. He was looking for your parents, all apologetic, wanting you back and hoping they would put in a good word for him."

Nervous tension rifled up her spine. "He didn't speak to them, did he?" she asked, distress edging her words.

He shook his head. "No, he found me first. We had a 'discussion' and came to a mutual agreement. While he won't be calling on you again, he also didn't tell me what happened. But I figured he stuffed up somehow and came begging your forgiveness."

Her brow creased and she crossed her arms, waiting for further explanation. "By 'discussion,' do you mean fight?"

No lies, just tell me the truth.

"Sort of. I mean he tried to deck me but it was pretty obvious he was not that good with his fists. All I was doing was defending myself, honest. He may have walked away with a black eye and a few bruised ribs. Nothing too drastic."

"Finn!" Cassidy sat staring out the window, processing his words, and her head started to pound. "I can't believe you did that."

"I know you've had a pretty trying day, but what happened between you two? The least you could do is fill your friend in on the details. Especially after I put my body on the line for you."

The air thickened and the last thing she wanted was for Todd to become a bigger thorn in her friendship with Finn. "Okay, let's get it out in the open once and for all." Cassidy saw Finn's hands clench the steering wheel, but she forged ahead. "Do you remember me telling you that Todd and I were supposed to attend his work dinner before I left?"

"Yes, I remember. You were so excited to be finally meeting his big bosses."

She huffed and folded her arms across her tightened chest. The pain of Todd's betrayal was a memory she hadn't wanted to relive. "I couldn't decide on a dress for the event, so I called in to see Todd at work, to get his opinion. But he wasn't there. Apparently, he was working in the downtown office that day. So, I went to see him there." She paused, swallowing back the nausea that threatened to surface. "Turns out he was in a 'meeting' with his boss' wife, and when I say meeting, I think you can guess what sort of meeting I'm talking about."

Finn's jaw clenched and he sucked in a deep breath. "Could you have been mistaken?"

"Mistaken? I hardly think so. I really don't want to have to explain what I saw. I'm sure you can guess. I was so embarrassed and I could just feel everyone laughing at me. What a fool I'd made of myself, especially in front of you."

"Me?" he asked with a raised eyebrow.

She shook her head, her mind full of horrible images of Todd and that woman. "You tried to warn me, but I didn't listen. I couldn't face you or my parents after I raved about how in love I was and that I'd met the man of my dreams. I was a gullible sucker who'd fallen for the image, not the real person." Cassidy gazed out the side window, her damp eyes threatening to expose her heartache.

"Todd was a fool to let you slip through his fingers," Finn said as he turned down her street. "That was his mistake. I should have given him two black eyes."

She gave a little giggle, imaging Todd walking into work with two black eyes and having to explain to his boss how he'd gotten them. "The fact that you defended me is something I will never forget. It means the world to me. Thank you," she said as she wiped her eyes, refusing to shed another tear over that man.

"I'll always have your back, you never have to ask," Finn said with a smile as he turned the ignition off.

Cassidy's tummy did a somersault and she held her breath a moment as his words washed over her. She'd never doubt his faith in her again. "Would you like to come in for a nightcap?"

"Sure."

Finn followed Cassidy down the hall and into the kitchen. The sweet aroma of hazelnut hung thick in the air, tickling her nose. *Clair's been at the coffee machine again.* They both jumped in unison, startled by Clair's voice behind them.

"There you are," Clair said as she popped her head around the corner, a mug of steaming coffee in hand. "What took you so long?"

"Yeah, sorry about that. The trip took a little longer than expected." Cassidy said, glaring at her sister and hoping she'd take the hint. Turning to Finn, she asked, "Coffee?"

"Love one," he said taking a seat at the table.

"So, tell me, Finn, which hotel are you staying at?" Clair asked as she joined him.

His eyes widened and he looked from Clair to Cassidy and back again. *Oh no, he hasn't booked a hotel yet.*

Finn cleared his throat. "Who needs a hotel, when I have my swag in the back of my Jeep? Best thing about travelling in Australia, you can pitch your tent just about anywhere."

Cassidy handed Finn his coffee and joined them at the table. "You always did say you liked to sleep under the stars."

"Guess the stars were hard to see in New York, amongst the buildings?" Clair said.

He shrugged. "Yeah, I guess. That's what makes my job exciting. I get to visit different, wonderful locations and meet amazing, interesting people. But I know none of it compares to what Australia has to offer."

His eyes sparkled as he glanced in Cassidy's direction as he spoke. His words held a double meaning that was not lost on her.

"Why pitch your tent, when we have a perfectly good spare room sitting waiting to be used? Cassidy would love to have you stay and I know Charlotte and I would feel a lot better if you hung around until this mess is sorted out," Clair said. Her sheepish gaze caught Cassidy's eye.

Why that little matchmaker. Her heart overflowed with love for her sister. Even though Cassidy was

114

facing a murder charge, her big sister still had time to play the guardian angel. *I can play along.*

"Yes, you may as well use the room," Cassidy said casually. "After all, it just sits there, empty. I'm surprised it doesn't have cobwebs growing in it from lack of use."

"What do you say, Finn?" Clair asked.

Finn smiled and placed his coffee mug down on the table. "I say...it sounds perfect."

Clair shot up like a firecracker and headed for the dishwasher. "Great, it's all settled."

"What's all settled?" Charlotte asked as she entered, placing her empty mug in the dishwasher.

Clair grinned at Charlotte. "We were just convincing Finn, here, to stay in the spare room instead of pitching his tent."

Charlotte clasped her hands together in agreement. "What a great idea. Besides, wouldn't you rather the comfort of a nice, king-sized bed, instead of the rocky earth under your body?"

Finn's eyes widened. "When you put it like that, how can I say no?"

Cassidy shook her head and her lips curled upward into a grin. *Oh, boy. You two are going to get it when I get five minutes alone with you.*

"I'm going to call it a night," Charlotte said heading toward the hallway. "I've Jessica's sixteenth birthday cake to complete and Pierre is only working a half day, as he is off to Sydney for a few days leave."

Gratitude bubbled in Cassidy's stomach and her throat clogged with built-up emotion. "Wait. Before you go," she said, standing to join them. "I just wanted to say thank you for believing in me and coming through tonight with Caroline. I didn't know what I was going to do."

Charlotte pulled Cassidy to her chest as tears welled in her eyes. "That's what sisters are for, You Big Wally." Within seconds, Clair had joined in and they were laughing and squeezing each other tight.

Finn's soft voice broke the moment. "If you three need a moment, I'm happy to step out for a few minutes."

"Oh, haha," Cassidy said, play-punching him in the bicep. *Oww, that hurt. When did his biceps become rocks?*

Clair chuckled and continued. "About tomorrow. I know Charlotte's busy at the shop and I know you've only just arrived in town, but I thought Cassidy and I could make a trip to the mayor's office. The sooner we get to the bottom of the scene between him and Christina at the gala dinner the better."

"Of course, you need to do what you have to do. What can I do to help?" he asked.

"I could use your muscles," Clair said with a chuckle.

Excuse me? Cassidy pulled back and raised an eyebrow at her sister.

"What I mean is, I am desperate to get CC's Cupcake Haven up and running as soon as possible and I know Cassidy is working on the final touches of her designs for the interior. I have Mason heading over to meet some contractors and Liam is working on the back landscaping. He could use an extra set of hands. Cassidy and I can meet you there after we finish chatting with the mayor. What do you say?"

"Clair!" Cassidy said, folding her arms across her chest, a frown marring her expression. "Finn did not come to stay just so you can put him to work." Cassidy's gut tightened when a bright shade of red coloured Clair's face.

"Hey, it's fine. I don't mind at all. In fact, it will be a great workout," Finn said, easing the tension. He placed a calming hand on Cassidy's shoulder and she felt it all the way to her big toe. "Honest, Cass, it's cool." Goose bumps assailed her body. She'd never had that reaction to his touch or his pet name for her before. Her feelings for Finn were changing in a big way, but was it a direction she wanted to take?

"Thank you," Clair said, a smile brimming from ear to ear. "Okay, good night. I'm going before Cassidy flattens me with her death stare."

Cassidy's jaw dropped, but before she could say a word, her gaze caught the wispy tendrils of Clair's red hair flitting out of the kitchen, closely followed by Charlotte.

"Night," Charlotte called over her shoulder.

"Thank you for offering to help out tomorrow," Cassidy said, still jittery from her unexpected reaction to his touch. "Follow me, I'll show you to the spare room." Finn followed and he was so close she could feel him shuffle up behind her. *Oh gosh, having Finn stay in the room opposite mine is going to be harder than I thought.*

"Are you sure you're okay with me staying?" Finn asked, his breath skimming her neck.

Noooooo, bellowed like an air siren blasting in her head. "Of course, no problem. It's the least I can do to say thank you for being there this evening." Reaching the door, she spun right into Finn's firm torso and her body fell back against the wall. She gasped and he made a grab for her before she landed on her backside on the tiled floor.

"Easy there," he said holding her still with his strong hands. A warm smile eased his lip up and the cutest dimple in his right cheek surfaced.

His cobalt-blue eyes held hers and for a moment she forgot to breathe. Cassidy's head swam with all the reasons why it shouldn't feel this good in his arms. One reason in particular. *Murder.* She shook off her thoughts and opened the door behind her. "Here we are. I hope this is okay?"

Finn followed her in and gazed around the room. It had a country charm to it, but mixed with a new, contemporary interior design, it would please even the fussiest house guest. "It's perfect," he said, his gaze glued to hers.

Cassidy ignored the butterflies in her stomach. "Great. I guess I'll see you in the morning," she said and headed out. "Do you need to grab anything from your car?"

He nodded. "Yes. You head off to bed, I'm sure I can find my way to the car and back again."

"You sure?"

"Absolutely," he said.

She smiled, nodded, and turned toward her room.

Thank goodness.

Chapter Nine

CASSIDY PLONKED HER foot on the dashboard as Clair headed to the top end of town, toward the mayor's house. Thankfully, Clair had the genius idea to ring ahead, otherwise, they'd be heading to an empty mayor's office in the council chambers instead of his home. "Glad you were on the ball this morning. It didn't even occur to me to ring before we left," Cassidy said, popping another piece of celery in her mouth.

"Do you mind?" Clair asked flicking her gaze between the road and Cassidy's foot on her dashboard.

Cassidy slid her foot off the dash, a soft blush warmed her cheeks. "Oh, sorry."

"What's with the celery stick?" Clair asked.

Cassidy shrugged, an innocent lie rolling sweetly off her tongue. "Just thought I should eat a little healthier these days. I swear I put on two dress sizes when I was in New York."

Clair's eyebrow rose. "Oh… I thought it might have had something to do with our new house guest."

Cassidy's head reared back. "What on earth are you talking about? Finn and I are just friends. Charlotte's health kick rubbed off on me, that's all."

"If you say so." Clair drove on in silence but a quirky smile skimmed her lips every now and then.

"By the way, it was pretty obvious you were playing matchmaker last night," Cassidy said.

Clair gasped and her hand flew to her heart as if Cassidy's words had sliced it in two. "Me? I did no such thing."

"Oh, come on, Clair," Cassidy said shuffling in her seat. "It was so obvious you were trying your best to convince him to stay." A fake horrified expression clouded Clair's eyes and Cassidy knew she'd hit a nerve.

"I would never. I just happened to think it's ridiculous to have a man sleep in a tent when there's a perfectly good bed available."

"I see." Scepticism seeped into Cassidy's tone.

Clair turned down the mayor's street. She giggled. "Of course, if it does happen to turn into something more than friendship, you can thank me later."

"Clair! Finn and I are just friends. How many times do I have to say it?" Frustration rooting itself in the base of her belly.

Clair cut the ignition of her car and held her hand up. "Okay, okay. I won't mention it again."

"Thank you. I'd appreciate that." *It's going to be hard enough without you putting your two cents in when you feel like playing matchmaker.*

They stopped at the ornately-designed, stained-glass door. "You ready?" Clair asked.

"Ready to prove my innocence? You betcha," Cassidy said as she rang the doorbell.

Within minutes, the door was flung open and they were staring into the pale, drawn face of Mayor Brad Windsor. Cassidy's eyes widened and she paused a moment, taking in his fatigued appearance. *This is not the Brad Windsor I remember.* "Mayor Windsor, we're so sorry to disturb you at home, but it's a matter of urgency that we speak with you."

"Clair… Cassidy, this really isn't a good time. Call my office and make an appointment," he said as he began to close the door.

Cassidy's stomach clenched and she could see her freedom slipping through her fingers. "No, it can't wait. Please, it's a matter of life and death. My life, anyway."

His brow creased and the light faded from his eyes. "I'm sorry, but I can't help you. As I said, now is not a good time."

"There never is a good time when it comes to murder," Clair said.

"Murder?

Clair paused, confused. He was the mayor. How would he have missed something so colossal as another murder? *Something is not right here.* "Christina Jacobs' murder. I'm sure you've heard that Cassidy is the number one suspect."

He shook his head as if to shift his focus and huffed. "Yes, I may have heard something to that effect."

Clair continued. "But there has been talk that you may have had something to do with her downfall."

He balked, his voice raising an octave. "Me?"

"Yes, and we'd hate to get the wrong information. You, of all people, know what bad publicity can do to a career being such a public figure. All we need is a few moments of your time," Cassidy asked, her raspy voice edged with desperation.

He sighed and opened the door. "Fine, but let's make it quick. I'm extremely busy today."

Funny. His receptionist said he called in sick. Cassidy and Clair nodded in unison and followed him into his home office.

He leant against the edge of his desk, his brow creased in obvious annoyance. "What's all this nonsense about?"

"Word has it, you had a very public incident on the dance floor of the gala dinner last month where you were overheard threatening Christina," Cassidy said in her best sleuthing tone.

His jaw tightened, but Clair chimed in before he had a chance for a rebuttal. "I think Christina's words were, 'I'll see you in hell' and you responded with, 'Not if I see you first.' That sounds like a threat to me."

"That was totally taken out of context," he said shooting off the desk. "Why would I waste my time killing her, when I could bring to light all her discrepancies through my connections at the council?"

He did have a point, Cassidy thought.

"I don't have time for this," he said, heading toward the front door.

It was at that moment Cassidy noticed the run-down state of the house. It wasn't like Sheryl to let things get so out of order. "I wonder if Detective Anderson would be interested in your conversation with Christina? After all, he didn't make it to the gala dinner and I'd hate him to get the story third hand."

He froze halfway to the front door. Cassidy caught Clair's eye and she shrugged at his static frame. *What is going on? This wasn't the Brad Windsor they elected to office.*

"That witch was going to blackmail me," he said as he slowly turned. His eyes were drawn and his expression suddenly defeated. "I've been keeping a secret from Ashton Point and somehow she found out. She may be the worst human being I have ever encountered, but if I killed her, it would take me away from Sheryl and she needs me now more than ever."

A bad feeling rooted itself deep in Cassidy's chest. She didn't like where this was headed. "You're not sick, are you?" Cassidy asked.

He shook his head and his eyes glistened. "No, I'm not sick." He paused. "Sheryl is."

Cassidy gasped. She hadn't seen the mayor's wife around town for months, but the last thing she'd ever imagined was that Sheryl was sick. Nausea filled her stomach.

"She has Alzheimer's and it's hit her hard and fast. We've been trying to deal with it ourselves, but I had no idea it would be so hard." Brad trudged back over to his office and the life drained out of his body as he sank into a chair by the entrance. "That woman." He shook his head. "That woman somehow found out about Sheryl's illness and thought it appropriate to tell me on the dance floor at the gala. Then she proceeded to blackmail me. She's a nasty piece of work. If I didn't resign as mayor and nominate her to join the council, she was going to crucify Sheryl in public, tell lies about her illness and make it known that I am unfit to continue my role as mayor, which is ludicrous. There is no way I'd let that woman say a single harsh word about Sheryl."

"Oh, Brad. I had no idea," Clair said a silent tear rolling down her cheek. "We were wrong, so wrong."

"You didn't know." He chuckled to himself. "I wanted to kill her, believe me, but I didn't. There would be no one to look after Sheryl if I went to prison."

Cassidy felt her cheeks redden with embarrassment and a pang of regret ripped through her. They'd stormed his house, his private sanctuary, throwing accusations around like they were the police themselves. *I'm no better than Daniel.* "I'm so sorry," Cassidy said, edging closer to the solemn figure. "What can we do to help?"

Clair nodded. "Yes, name it."

His broken gaze stared right through them and his lips turned up into a semi-smile. "You're sweet, both of you. But you have enough to worry about without adding my burden to your list. All I ask is that you keep Sheryl's condition quiet. I'm organising some in-house nursing and I only have three months left in office. When she was first diagnosed, we discussed it and agreed that I would complete my stint as mayor. She made me promise and if I'm nothing else, I'm a man of my word."

Cassidy's heart broke in two. "Count on it. No-one will hear about it from us. Right, Clair?"

"Right. And you can expect regular cupcake deliveries to help keep you both smiling."

He rose and Cassidy felt her body plunge forward as he grabbed both of them in his arms and held on tight. "Thank you, your word means the world to me. I may have my hands full, but if I can help out in any way with clearing your name, let me know." Relief filled her core when he finally released them. "I'm just so happy that you three girls have settled down with nice men and are making lives for yourselves."

"Excuse me," Cassidy said with a raised eyebrow. "Settled down?"

He nodded. "Yes, Alison called earlier regarding some council business and she happened to mention that your boyfriend was there last night. I knew Clair and Charlotte were spoken for, but I had no idea that you had joined them."

"I have!?"

Annoyance ran rife through Cassidy's body as she sat beside Clair. *How dare Finn think he can go around telling everyone he's my boyfriend? Of all the sneaky, underhanded things to do.* As if she needed the hassle of a boyfriend, especially after her experience with Todd. As far as she was concerned, Finn was a friend. She was off dating men.

"Are you okay?" Clair asked, breaking her chain of thought.

"No, not really. I just can't understand why Finn would do that," she said, dropping her head back on the headrest.

Clair shrugged. "Maybe he had a good reason. I can think of two right now."

Cassidy's breath caught sharply in her throat and she glared at her sister. "Oh, really? And what might they be?"

"For starters, it doesn't take a genius to work out that Finn is sweet on you. He may have said he was passing by Ashton Point, but when you think about it, what man follows his 'friend' all the way from New York to Australia, just to find out why she didn't say goodbye? Unless he already had feelings for her, feelings that were more than friendship. He could have just called you by phone and asked but he didn't. He came in person." Clair paused and took a deep breath.

More than friendship? The pieces of the puzzle seemed to fall into place, like they'd been there all along behind an invisible wall that had just been demolished. Finn had warned her about Todd and he'd been standoffish when she'd blabbed about how smart Todd was and about his job on Wall Street. All the while, it must have been awful for him to endure her schoolgirl antics. Cassidy dropped her head in her hands and groaned, remembering the cold reception she'd gotten from Finn every time she mentioned

Todd's name. Nausea worked its way into the back of her throat. *How embarrassing.*

"Or…he could have just stretched the truth so they would let him in to see you last night," Clair added casually.

What the…? Her head snapped and her gaze focussed on the road ahead. "Yes, that must be it. I don't even want to think about your first option."

"Why on earth not? He's cute."

Her head began to pound under the drone of Clair's voice. "Exactly. And remember what happened to the last cute guy I met. He chewed my heart up and spat it out, without a care in the world. I'm not in a hurry to jump back into the dating game. I just want to focus on two things, me not going to prison and my work. Can we do that, please?"

"Sure, if you say so," Clair said.

"I know you're heading out to the Sweets place and then on to see Alex at the hot springs, but do you think you could drop me home first? Thanks to this murder business, I'm running behind with the final touches for the new shop."

"Sure. This change wouldn't have something to do with Finn, would it?"

Cassidy sat in silence, stone-faced, the throbbing pain in her head increasing by the second.

After a moment, Clair continued. "Okay, no more questions. There's only one problem. By now, half the town will probably know you're dating."

Great, can this day get any worse?

Chapter Ten

FINN JUMPED OUT of his car and bolted to Cassidy's front door, his whole body still reeling from his absentmindedness. *How could I have been so stupid?* Forgetting to tell Cassidy what he'd said to Alison last night at the police station could destroy her trust in him. He wasn't deceitful like Todd.

He'd slogged away all morning and into the early afternoon with Liam, working up a good sweat under the intense Australian sun. It was good to work out doing manual labour instead of at the gym. Finn smiled when he saw Clair's car pull up, but his enjoyment quickly faded when she got out alone. Once Clair explained what happened at the mayor's house and Cassidy's absence, he couldn't get to her quick enough to explain.

He sucked in a deep breath of salty air and rapped his knuckles against the stained-glass door.

His heart sank when the door flew open and Cassidy greeted him. The hurt in her eyes ripped his heart in two. Hurt he'd caused.

"Well, if it isn't the boyfriend I didn't even know I had," she said with disdain.

Finn's gut clenched. "Let me explain. Please?"

Cassidy shrugged. "If you must, but it's no big deal." She turned back down the hallway, toward the lounge room.

"It is a big deal, to me, anyway." Their friendship was too important to let a little misunderstanding come between them. "It's not what you think," he said following her into the house.

"Oh, and what do I think?" she asked snuggling into the corner of the couch. "Do you always go around lying and making up fake girlfriends when it suits you?"

He joined her on the couch, unable to bear the distance between them. He hated the barrier she'd erected. "No, absolutely not. The last thing I ever wanted to do was hurt you. I didn't deliberately keep it from you. After everything that happened at the police station and then when we got back you started to open up about Todd, it kinda just slipped my mind."

"Pretty big thing to have slipped your mind. Especially in a small town like Ashton Point, where the town folk thrive on gossip."

The hurt in her voice gutted him. "I know and I'm sorry. I don't make a habit of lying, but they weren't going to let me in to see you and I knew I had to be there for you. It was the first thing that popped into my head. I'm so sorry, Cass." She sat as still as a statue and his stomach churned. Had he blown it for good? "I know after everything that happened with Todd you probably don't trust easily, but I'm not Todd and I would never intentionally hurt you. You mean more to me than that."

Her soft blue eyes shot to his and his breath caught in his throat at the tears threatening to drop. "What do you mean?" she asked.

"Like I said yesterday, Todd was crazy to let you slip through his fingers. I've done a pretty good job of keeping my feelings for you hidden, but if we're being totally honest, I like you. I have since the day we met in the apartment foyer in New York."

Cassidy gasped and her mouth rounded in an O. "I had no idea."

"You weren't supposed to. You were in love with Todd. Who was I to come between true love?" he asked.

She closed her eyes and squeezed her arms tight around her body. "Don't remind me. Some love, huh?"

"I'm just glad you saw him for what he really was before it was too late. You no longer have to deal with him," Finn said, easing back on the couch.

"I'm glad too." Cassidy paused, biting her lower lip. "Finn…about your feelings for me."

He smiled and held up his hand. "It's okay, Cass, you don't have to reciprocate. I just wanted you to know how I felt."

She frowned. "No, that's not it. You see, I don't know if what I feel for you is friendship or something more. I enjoy your company and when I'm around you, you make me happy. But my future is so uncertain and I may be facing a life behind bars, if I can't work out who killed Christina. I'm not prepared to open my heart to another relationship until I know for sure where my life is headed. I understand why you did what you did last night and I appreciate it. For now, I could use a friend. At least 'til I get my life in order. Can you understand?"

Adrenaline danced up his spine. *I make her happy?* Finn's heart did a little somersault. He could do friendship. He'd be the best friend she'd ever have. If she happened to fall in love with him in the process, that would be an added bonus. "Of course. If a friend is what you need, then a friend is what you'll have." He watched the light return to her expression and he smiled. *I did that.*

"Thank you."

Cassidy's eyes flew open. She bolted upright on the couch with a start, her head spinning. "Awww,"

she said, rubbing the kink in her neck. "That'll teach me to do work on the lounge instead of the table."

After her chat with Finn, she'd settled into putting the final touches on her interior designs for CC's Cupcake Haven. Judging by the scattered mess of drawings on the floor and the crook in her neck, she'd fallen asleep. Her drawings had borne the brunt of her afternoon snooze.

She gathered her designs and put them back in the folder. The unusual stillness in the house didn't sit well with her. "Finn," she called waiting for his calming voice to answer. Silence. *Where are you?* She stood and headed into the kitchen, her bleary head and tastebuds in need of a coffee fix. "Finn, are you here?" Her words were met with continued silence.

Cassidy grabbed a Nespresso pod from the cupboard. Halfway across the kitchen, her eye caught movement in the backyard through the kitchen window. *Holy cow.* Her breath caught in the back of her throat and a sizzling blush worked its way up her neck to her cheeks.

She knew Finn worked out, but she'd never seen it in person. He was leaning against one of the garden chairs, his body in plank position and hard as rock while he did push-ups...shirtless and sweaty. Her jaw dropped and she couldn't take her eyes off his toned upper body. *How have I not known what a sexy body he hid under his clothes?*

A thunderous knocking on the front door startled her and she jumped about two feet in the air as if the floor were burning hot coals. She gasped and her hand flew to her chest. "Seriously? Way to give a woman a heart attack." She glanced one last time at the yummy view out the window, then trudged toward the front door, the image of Finn's half-naked body still at the forefront of her mind. Opening the door, her thoughts of Finn vanished as she looked into the worrying eyes of her friend Beth.

"Beth. Are you okay? You look like you've seen a ghost," Cassidy said, ushering her inside.

"Cassidy, thank goodness you're home," Beth said in a frantic tone. Her hands twisted into knots at her waist. "I didn't know if you'd be here, I just knew I had to find you."

"What on earth is going on?" Cassidy asked as she showed her into the kitchen. Both women stopped in their tracks, their eyes glued to Finn's shirtless body as he gulped down mouthfuls of water. Cassidy's pulse began to race and a smirk turned up the corner of her mouth. The view was definitely better close up. *Focus.*

She shook her head. "Finn." His head turned at the sound of her voice. "Good to see you've finished your workout, but we have company. Do you think you might put a shirt on?" His gaze turned downward to his half-naked body and his cheeks turned the cutest shade of crimson red.

"Please excuse me," he said, reaching for the shirt tucked into the back pocket of his shorts. "I didn't realise we had company."

"Finn, this is Beth, one of our dearest friends and newlyweds. Charlotte designed and created the most amazing cake for her wedding." Cassidy's stomach dropped when her focus returned to Beth.

She was as agitated as a poor animal locked in a cage. "Let's sit and then you can tell me what's got you so jumpy."

Beth took the seat next to Cassidy and paused a moment before speaking in the softest voice. "Is it okay to talk in front of him?"

Finn sidled up beside Cassidy and her back stiffened. His musky, sweaty scent played havoc with her senses.

"I'm sorry if I made you feel uncomfortable, Beth. That was not my intention," he said, finally joining them on the opposite side of the table. "Cassidy and I became friends when she was in New York. Her parents live in the same apartment building as I was staying. You could say I've grown pretty fond of her in the past few months and I will do anything to protect her. I know about Christina and how Detective Anderson is convinced Cassidy murdered her, but if you have information that can clear her name, please tell us."

Man, you're smooth. Cassidy all but melted at his heartfelt words and she sensed the ease that worked its way across the room. "Finn is on our side. Now, what is going on?"

Beth took a deep breath and began. "I'm not sure if you know, but Lincoln and I are starting our own landscaping business and we have been really working hard on saving money."

"Wait, is that the Lincoln that Liam is working for?" Finn asked. Beth nodded and Cassidy shushed him.

"I was over at our accountant's and I overheard Emmerson talking to someone. She was furious that Christina hadn't returned what she'd stolen from her. And then she said, 'Over my dead body will I let Christina destroy my future.'"

Finn and Cassidy looked at each other for a split second.

Beth continued, her voice an octave higher. "She said Christina got exactly what she had coming to her. It freaked me out and made me wonder what Christina had done to Emmerson to make her say such a thing. Just before I was about to go into Mr

Bancroft's office, she said death was not going to stop her from taking back what's hers."

Cassidy couldn't believe her luck and excitement danced in her veins. "Did Emmerson know you were there?"

Beth shook her head. "No, I don't think so. She was in the next room. I was a last-minute squeeze in. I wasn't supposed to be there. I know she's trying to get some money together to start her fashion business and sometimes helps out at her dad's office."

"Do you know who she was talking to?" Finn asked, a frown creased his brow.

"No, I couldn't really hear anyone. Maybe she was on the phone, I'm not sure." Her voice was as shaky as her hands. "The only thing I could think of was to get to you as soon as possible. I know you didn't do this, but what if Emmerson did?"

"Although it sounds suspicious, we can't be certain that she had anything to do with Christina's murder. For now, I think we should keep it between us, at least until we get some concrete evidence to prove her innocence or her guilt."

Beth thought on Cassidy's words for a moment. "I suppose you're right. I know we don't have to report it, but don't you think we should tell the police?"

Frustration bubbled in Cassidy's belly. "Tell them what? All we have is a conversation that has Emmerson saying death won't stop her getting back what's hers. She said Christina got what she had coming to her, but I can name a few other residents of Ashton Point who feel exactly the same."

Beth nodded. "I suppose you're right."

Cassidy wrapped Beth's cold, trembling hands in hers and smiled. "Trust me, Beth. Finn and I will look into it. This isn't your fight but thank you. You've given us a new lead to follow."

"Really?"

Cassidy nodded. "Yes, really."

Chapter Eleven

"YOU CAN'T BE serious," Finn said as he paced the kitchen, frustration eating away at his insides.

Cassidy stood with her spine ram-rod straight and her hands on her hips. "It's the perfect plan, don't you see? We go over, under the pretence of showing interest in her fashion business and maybe offering her some work. Beth said she's trying to get some money together to start a business. She'd probably be happy to have the chance at another source of income."

Finn ran his hand through his damp hair. "Wouldn't a better option be to tell Detective Anderson?"

Cassidy pursed her lips together. "No, we can't. There isn't enough to go on yet. What can we say except that Beth overheard a conversation and then told me? He'd probably laugh me out of the station or worse, arrest me for interfering in a police investigation."

Finn shook his head. "I don't like it, and neither would your sisters."

Cassidy rolled her cute blue eyes to the roof and Finn's chest tightened. "Pfft, my sisters would want me to do what's necessary to clear my name, goodness knows they did when they were in the same predicament. Are you with me?" she asked, her eyes widening as if seeking his approval.

Cassidy's determination was one of the qualities that made her stand out from the rest of the women he'd met. "Do I have a choice?" he said with a sigh.

She shook her head and grinned from ear to ear. "No, not really. Let's go."

Finn balked at her rushed command. "What…now?"

"Yes, now. The sooner, the better," she said, grabbing her bag from the hall stand.

I stink, I can't go out like this. I even offend myself after a workout. "Give me ten minutes to have a shower. Surely, you can hold off that long. Why don't you ring your sisters and fill them in on what we've learned from Beth and I promise I'll be done before you're finished."

Cassidy folded her arms across her chest and squinted at him. "Done before I'm finished, hey?"

"Promise," he said and headed double-time toward the bathroom.

Finn moved at lightning speed and was in and out of the shower in record time. He shouldn't have bothered, as he was just as hot and sweaty from rushing as he had been before the shower. The mugginess of the late summer afternoon hadn't helped. At least he was in clean clothes. He finished buttoning the top button of his shirt as he entered the kitchen.

Cassidy's sweet voice still hummed away on the phone. He paused by the doorway, soaking in the sight of the red-headed beauty sitting with her back to him. He loved everything about her, the way she moved and the way she sat, talked, giggled. He wanted her in his life, and not just as a friend. A groan escaped his throat. *Oh gosh, I sound like one of those men in a soppy romance movie.*

Finn opened his mouth to speak and his heart did a double take at the mention of his name. "Yes, Clair, Finn is coming with me," she said, sarcasm seeping through her tone. "No, Clair, I won't… Yes, Clair… Yes… He's in the shower …Clair! Stop that right now."

Stop what? And what did it have to do with my shower? He could stand and watch her all day. It was like watching the Energizer Bunny in action, but much easier on the eye. He took a step forward and cleared his throat. Her head spun.

She gasped and shot from her chair. "Clair, I have to go. Will you pass the information on to Charlotte for me? …Yes, we'll be careful. Thanks, bye." She hung up and glared in his direction. "How long have you been standing there?" she asked.

The wrong answer here could land him in hot water. *Play it safe.* "Not long, but I was right. I did make it out before you finished your phone calls, and by the sounds of it, you only made one."

Cassidy picked up her bag and headed for the door. Finn moved close behind. "By the time I told Clair what Beth had said, she morphed into the worrying 'big sister' mode again, giving me the warning speech."

"I'm sure she just worries about you. I know I do," he said before he could call the words back.

She threw her arms up in the air in an exasperated sigh. "Great, now you sound like my big brother."

He balked. *Big brother!* That's the last person he wanted to be. "Believe me, my feelings for you are far from brotherly," he said to himself. Finn wasn't sure if she'd heard him, but her head lowered and he could have sworn he saw her cheeks turn a shade that matched her hair colour.

Finn drove and they made comfortable small talk, neither addressing the comment he'd made as they left the house.

"That's Emmerson," Cassidy said pointing to the car exiting a driveway ahead.

"Are you sure?" he asked, slowing the car.

"Trust me. I'd know that black VW Beetle anywhere. It's not like there are many in town."

Good enough for me. He gripped the steering wheel. "I'm assuming we're following her?"

Cassidy giggled. "Follow that car," she said, pointing out the windscreen. "I've always wanted to say that. Although now that I have, I feel kinda silly."

Finn's brain was screaming to stay focused on the task ahead. His heart swelled at the sight of Cassidy's cheeky grin, which made her blue eyes seem even bigger than usual. Finn reeled his thoughts in before they led him in a direction he dared not tread. "Where do you think she's going?"

She shrugged, her eyes focused on Emmerson's vehicle ahead. "Beats me, but she appears to be heading toward the river."

Finn drove a safe distance away, his eyes glued to the dainty black car. It veered toward what appeared to be an expensive area and he eased his foot off the gas pedal when he heard Cassidy gasp. "What is it?"

"She's heading toward Christina Jacobs' house."

"Really?" *Why would she be going there?* He watched Emmerson pull up out front of what he assumed was the Jacobs house. "Is that Christina's house?"

Cassidy kind of nodded and pointed in Emmerson's direction. "Look, she's not heading into the parent's retreat. She's walking toward Christina's house."

"I don't think it matters that much, why would you openly park in front of a murder scene, unless you wanted people to think you were trying to hide something? Or worse, retrieve something." He pulled over to the side of the road behind a caravan, his Jeep Wrangler perfectly hidden by the over-sized luxury vehicle.

"Good point," Cassidy said rummaging around in her handbag. "Bingo." The clanging of keys nabbed his focus. She was dangling a set of house keys in front of his face. "I totally forgot I had these. Christina demanded I give them back, but it slipped my mind and then she was…you know."

"Murdered," he said.

"Yes. I have a plan." Her eyes glowed with anticipation. "We follow her into Christina's house. We have to find out what Emmerson is doing in there. It could be the link to proving my innocence."

"Technically…you don't have permission to enter," he said sarcastically. "The police won't look kindly on us snooping around in Christina's house, even if it isn't officially a crime scene."

She sighed and rolled her eyes once more. "Only if we get caught and we won't."

Finn rubbed his chin in thought. "I don't like it. Breaking the law isn't on my bucket list."

She sighed. "I know, mine neither, but I'd do just about anything to prove my innocence. And, you never know we might find the answers the police need to solve the murder. What do you say?"

"What if she *is* the murderer? We have no idea what she might do when she sees us."

"That's why I have you, you big lug," she said, punching his upper arm. "Between you and me I'm sure we'd be able to defend ourselves against the likes of Emmerson Bancroft. Besides, you're the big one, I can always hide behind you. We can't just sit here and do nothing."

She batted her eyelids at him and he was a goner. She was right about one thing, he would protect her. With his life if he had to. "Okay, you win, but let's not go in guns blazing. Quiet and with caution, agreed?"

She nodded. "Agreed."

Cassidy's pulse raced as they stood at Christina's door, ready to enter. "Wait," she whispered, her hand on his shoulder paused his step.

"What?" he mouthed.

She continued, her voice barely audible. "We should turn our phones on silent. The last thing we need is a phone call alerting her to our presence." He nodded in agreement. She held her breath as he eased the front door open. The lock had been picked. *How does Emmerson know how to pick a lock?* She leaned forward, squinting to see around his big frame. "Go," she whispered. Adrenaline buzzed inside her belly.

He nodded. Cassidy felt like a lioness stalking her pray as she crept inside the house. Her senses were on high alert and picked up a rustling sound coming from Christina's lounge room. Finn made a shushing gesture with his finger and then pointed toward the source of the noise. They both nodded in unison. She felt an icy chill crawl up her spine at the knowledge that less than a week ago, a murder happened in the retreat next door.

As she stepped into the lounge room, her sightline was immediately drawn to the activity by the back wall. She watched Emmerson rummage through the sideboard cupboard, her size eight backside sticking up in the air, oblivious to their presence.

What are you looking for? She saw the confused expression on Finn's face. Cassidy had the element of surprise on her side. She looked at Finn and mouthed, *one, two, three.* "Looking for something?" she asked, shattering the semi-quiet room.

Emmerson sprang upright like a Jack-in-the-box at a child's birthday party. Her eyes widened as she took in the tall, commanding Finn standing to Cassidy's left. "Cassidy, what are you doing here?"

"I think a more appropriate question is, what are you doing here?" she said her confidence growing by the second.

Emmerson paled and her eyes began to moisten. "I-I-I lent Christina a pair of shoes and I just came to get them back."

"Really? From the sideboard in her lounge room? I would have thought you would find shoes in the bedroom. What do you think, Finn?"

"That's where I keep mine," he said, his gaze drilling Emmerson to the spot.

"Maybe you were looking for something else, something that might incriminate you in Christina's murder. I mean that's the only reason I can think of that you would break into a dead woman's house less than a week after she was murdered." Within seconds, Emmerson crumbled and fell into the nearby armchair, her watering eyes now harbouring floods of tears that rolled down her cheeks.

"No, no, no. You've got it all wrong," she said between hiccups. "I know this looks bad, but I didn't kill Christina. Yes, I admit I broke in, but it's not what you think."

Cassidy frowned. "What are you looking for?" Her heart softened a fraction as she took in Emmerson's mascara running down her reddened cheeks. Honest distress brimmed in her eyes.

Emmerson sighed realising defeat. "Photographs."

"Photographs." Finn and Cassidy said in unison.

Emmerson nodded. "Yes, photographs of me when I was about seventeen. I was visiting my cousin in Melbourne. We got a little drunk one night and took some rather revealing pictures. We were silly teenagers just mucking around. I had no idea that she'd uploaded them to her computer."

Confusion muddled Cassidy's mind. "What do these pictures have to do with Christina's death?"

"She found them. I don't know how, but she found them." Emmerson's tears began to flow like a torrent once more. "She was going to blackmail me. She called me the night before she was murdered and she threatened me with running the pictures on the front page of *The Chronicle* if I didn't do something for her. I asked what, but she wouldn't tell me over the phone."

Blackmail? Just like Mayor Windsor. Cassidy didn't like to think the worst of the dead, but her chest tightened as her loathing for Christina grew.

Emmerson's hysterical voice hit an octave Cassidy had never experienced before. "I don't know, she didn't say. She was going to tell me when we met and then she was murdered and now I have no idea what she did with the photos or where they are."

"Sounds like motive for murder to me," Finn said, his sharp tone notching the tension between them up a level.

Emmerson's eyes widened and her jaw fell open in shock. "No, no, no. I wasn't even in Ashton Point that night. I was in Sydney. I was following up with some contacts for my new fashion business and then I met this guy and we had dinner and took in a movie."

"But you could have come back in plenty of time to commit the murder," he added.

Emmerson stood, her chocolate-brown eyes focused solely on Finn. "Yes, I could have, but I didn't. I ended up staying in Sydney overnight. I left about eight in the morning, I even have a speeding ticket just as I left the Sydney CBD to prove it. There was no way I could have killed Christina. If I killed her, I'd never find out what she did with the pictures."

Emmerson's story seemed pretty solid. Cassidy's heart plummeted. *Another dead end.* "I'm sorry for jumping to the wrong conclusion. If it's any consolation, when I was working next door, I didn't find any revealing photos of you. Rest assured that if I do hear of any, you'll be the first to know."

The corners of Emmerson's lip turned up into a semi-smile. "Thank you. I would hate for my father to find out. It could ruin his business, not to mention the one I'm trying to get off the ground. And for what it's worth, I believe you had nothing to do with her murder either."

By the time they left, Cassidy's hopes had deflated. The venture had turned out to be a total fizzer. They'd eliminated Emmerson from the murder list but were no closer to finding the real killer. "That didn't exactly go as I thought it would," Cassidy said, dumping her bag on the coffee table and collapsing into the corner of the lounge with a sigh. The empty house added to her depressed state.

"I know. I guess we need to keep looking for answers," Finn said, easing himself down beside her.

She felt a pang of panic in her chest. "Or until my time runs out."

"Hey," Finn snapped, a frown crossed his expression. He grabbed her hands in his. Startled by his quick movement, she sat there staring into the depths of his cobalt-blue eyes. "That will be enough of that defeated talk, thank you. I'm not giving up and neither should you. I happen to think you have a long and happy future ahead."

Finn's words were like a lifebuoy holding her afloat in the treacherous ocean, supporting her as he'd always done. His hypnotising gaze, combined with his manly aftershave, had her stomach doing flip-flops. Cassidy's gaze dropped to his lips.

What I wouldn't give to have you kiss me right now. She could no longer ignore her feelings for him, but how could she start a relationship with so much uncertainty hanging over her head?

He rubbed his soothing thumbs across the back of her hands. "I think you know my feelings for you."

"Why didn't you tell me before now?" she asked. She already knew the answer. "Todd."

He nodded. "I could tell he wasn't right for you, but I also couldn't lose your friendship. Can I ask you one question, Cass? And I want you to be honest with me." He said in a soft but caring tone.

"Of course."

"If Todd hadn't come on the scene and I'd asked you out, do you think you may have said yes?"

Would I? She paused, her mind racing through the countless times they spent together in New York. Movie nights on the couch, popcorn fights, shopping sprees, cooking lessons at his expense. All of which had filled her with happiness. A happiness she wanted to experience again and again and again. She wanted Finn, of that she had no more doubt. "Yes. I would have said yes."

He smiled and her heart melted. "Then how about when this nightmare is all over and we prove your innocence, you and I go on a real date? No pressure, just two people who like spending time together."

She nodded and her chest tightened as Finn leaned in toward her. She felt her breath catch in her throat. His soft lips on hers. He didn't force the kiss, but he didn't have too, she felt it all the way to the bottom of her soul. She savoured the sweet taste of him committing it to memory.

"Ah-hum." A deep, throaty cough from the hallway interrupted the moment.

She pulled back, her hands sliding from his. Cassidy's cheeks warmed under Liam's gaze. *How did I not hear him come in?* She caught Finn's lip curl into a grin. *Cheeky man.* "Liam, what an unexpected surprise."

"Yeah, sorry, didn't mean to interrupt your moment. I pulled up at the same time as Clair and she gave me her key to get in since she was on the phone.

Guess I should have knocked," he said, his face turning beetroot red.

"Don't be silly. Finn and I were just—"

Liam squeezed his eyes shut and held up his hand. "Please, I don't need to know. Information overshare."

A giggle erupted in Cassidy's belly and worked its way up into her throat. "Oh, don't be silly. I was going to say that Finn and I were just clearing the air."

"Riiiiight. Whatever you say." Liam flopped down on the opposite armchair. "Listen, there was a reason I called in. Finn, I was wondering if you have a couple of hours spare this evening? I could really do with an extra pair of hands to finish a decking job for a private client. We've at least a few hours of light left and I had someone lined up but they fell through."

Finn raised his brow and glanced at Cassidy. "Would you mind?"

Why would I mind? It's not like we're a couple. At least not yet. "Of course not. Daylight savings can be a godsend, why waste it?"

"Waste what?" Clair said as she walked into the lounge room.

"The light," Liam said.

"What light?" Clair asked, her gaze searching each one of their faces for answers. She looked so confused that Cassidy lost it and fell back in fits of laughter.

Clair huffed and rolled her eyes to the roof then turned to Liam. "I thought you were out with Charlotte?"

"I was, but I had to drop her at the shop. Suzi called and apparently, she had an emergency order that needed Charlotte's help. Since we have a few hours of light left, I have a job I could finish tonight and could use Finn's help."

Cassidy could practically see the lightbulb flick on in Clair's head. "Ah, that light," Clair said.

Liam nodded and stood. "So, what do you say, Finn?"

"Sounds great. Let me just grab some old clothes." He turned to Cassidy and eased his warm hand over hers. "I'm only a phone call away if you need me."

"Thank you."

Chapter Twelve

CASSIDY WAVED AND shut the door behind the guys as they left and headed into the kitchen. A feeling of contentment worked its way into her heart.

Is this what it feels like to be in love? How would I know, she thought chuckling to herself. She could hardly call what she had with Todd love. All she knew was what she felt for Finn was so much better.

"Okay, young lady, spill," Clair said as she put a hazelnut Nespresso pod in the coffee machine.

A frown marred Cassidy's expression. *Is she talking about Emmerson or Finn?*

"I know something happened between you and Finn. A guy doesn't hold your hand and look into your eyes the way he did unless there's something there. Sisters tell each other everything, so come on out with it."

Cassidy's pulse sped up and she licked her lips at the memory of Finn's kiss. The sweet taste of his soft lips cemented in her heart.

Now sitting at the kitchen table, Clair patted the seat next to her. "Come, sit. Please don't make me ask again."

There was no way she was getting out of this kitchen tonight without filling Clair in on the details. "All right." Cassidy gave in and joined her at the table. "Finn and I came to an agreement this evening."

Clair raised her eyebrows. "And?"

"And, there's no use starting a relationship while I have a murder charge hanging over my head, but…"

"But?" Clair asked, hopefully.

"But. I can't deny how he makes me feel. I like him, Clair. I like him a lot and he likes me." A thrill danced up her spine. "He kissed me and it was so amazingly tender. Probably the best kiss I've ever had."

A grin spread across Clair's face and she clasped her hands together at her chest. "I'm so happy for you. You two are perfect together. So, what now?"

"We both agreed to wait until this whole Christina mess is sorted out. That way we can start fresh."

"Good idea," Clair said as she threw her arms around Cassidy and squeezed. "I love you."

"I love you too."

With all the talk of Finn, Cassidy had nearly forgotten about the eventful day she'd had. Releasing Clair, she said, "Now that we have the mushy stuff out of the way, would you like to know what else Finn and I uncovered today?"

Clair's spine stiffened and her eyes widened. "Definitely."

Cassidy launched into the day's events, barely taking a breath between sentences.

"Now Emmerson is off the list I'm not sure where that leaves us." Clair stood and paced the kitchen, her frustration radiating through her words. "Oh, that woman. It wasn't enough that she meddled in so many lives when she was alive, now she's doing it from the grave."

From the grave? Cassidy froze, the memory of a similar conversation played out in her mind. One that included their least favourite newspaper reporter. "Do you remember when we went to see Daniel?"

"Yes…why?" she asked.

"Don't you find it strange that Daniel said pretty much the exact same thing as Emmerson? I think you made the point that he didn't have to fabricate information, as his contract would be void since Christina's dead, and he said, 'I wish.' Maybe Christina was blackmailing him as well." Cassidy's mind raced. Adrenaline pumped her energy levels up as her deductive skills worked overtime. "There could have been something in his contract that she was holding over him. His alibi for the time of her murder was pretty flimsy at best. At home, alone."

"Wait a minute, you have the same alibi," Clair said, draining the last droplets from her coffee cup.

"Yes, but we know *I* didn't do it," Cassidy said, her hand covering her heart innocently. "I really feel another conversation with Daniel is in order. If he has nothing to hide, then his story will be the same. But he might crumble when we bring blackmail into the conversation. What do you say, you up for it?"

Clair glanced at the wall clock. "Okay, but can we take separate cars? Alex rang just as I arrived home and she's having man trouble. I was going to head over to visit her once I touched base with you and then continue on to see Mason. Two cars will mean I don't have to double back to drop you home."

"Sounds good to me." Cassidy threw her bag over her shoulder. Her keys dangled in her hand. "After we're done, I'll give Finn a call and maybe I can pick him up if he's finished up with Liam."

Clair grinned. "Sounds like a plan."

Cassidy eased her car into the bay behind Clair's red Toyota and then joined her on the sidewalk. "He's still here," she said, gesturing toward Daniel's white Hyundai. "Talk about a workaholic."

"Where else would he be?" Clair asked. She slid her hand over the cool door handle and pushed. No luck. Tapping her knuckles on the door she called, "Daniel... Daniel are you there?"

Impatience wormed its way into Cassidy's gut. "How long does it take to open the door?" Clair tapped again, more forcefully this time.

The door flung open, the noise startling the Rosella's nestling in the trees three shops down. Daniel's eyes widened when his gaze fell on Cassidy. "Come to give me my front-page story?"

I'll give you a front-page story, but it may not be exactly what you want to hear. "That all depends on you," she said with confidence.

"Me? What are you talking about?"

Clair piped up. "I suppose it depends on whether you think blackmail is a front page worthy story."

Cassidy saw the blood drain from his face and the dumbfounded expression confirmed her suspicions. He was hiding something.

"What's blackmail got to do with anything?" he asked in a semi-defeated voice.

"Blackmail can be such a nasty business. It's the innocent people who always suffer. Wouldn't you agree, Clair?"

Clair nodded. "Oh, definitely."

Spurred on by her growing confidence, she continued, "I'd hate to see blackmail be your undoing. Daniel, don't you think it would be in both our interests to clear the air?" It was as if the life drained from his body right in front of her. *Bingo.* "Was Christina blackmailing you?" Daniel stood stock still and Cassidy wasn't even sure if he was breathing.

"I'll talk, but not out here." He held the door open for the girls and they followed him into the foyer of *The Chronicle*. Daniel sat on the corner sofa, his head lowered and his hands glued together and shaking.

Why is he so nervous? Maybe he is about to confess. Cassidy stiffened, her senses on high alert.

"What I said to you last time you were here was the honest-to-God truth, I did not kill Christina. But you're right, she was blackmailing me."

"I knew it," Cassidy said. She wanted to jump up and high five the air but seeing Daniel's miserable expression she contained herself. "Why don't you start from the beginning?"

"You better sit down, then. This could take a while," he said, nodding toward the empty chairs.

Clair's eyes widened and she took a seat, leaving Cassidy standing. *Don't start without me.* She settled in the chair next to Clair. "Okay, we're listening."

"A few years back, before I moved to Ashton Point and before I got my career sorted, I was mixed up with the wrong crowd. Drugs and alcohol. It wasn't a pretty sight, let me tell you. I couldn't go a day without a drink or two or three. Anyway, one night I had a fight with my old man and drank more than I should have and…"

His voice trailed off and Cassidy's heart clenched when she caught the tear rolling down his cheek. She had a bad feeling about what was coming but didn't interrupt.

"I stole his car keys and stormed out of the house. I never made it to my mate's place. Instead I rolled the car and hit a tree." He paused as if building the courage to continue.

"Oh, Daniel, I'm so sorry," Clair said softly. "At least you weren't killed."

His voice dropped an octave and a sudden chill filled the room. "No, I wasn't, but the teenage girl I hit didn't make it."

Cassidy's stomach revolted and she thought she might be sick. Clair's hand darted to her hand and she gripped it so hard Cassidy thought the blood had stopped circulating.

"Clair," she whispered. "Do you mind?" she nodded toward her frozen hand.

Clair's gaze followed hers. "Oh, sorry." She snapped her hand back and focused on Daniel once more. "I can't tell you how sorry we are. That was the old Daniel. The Daniel we know is smart, kind and may occasionally print an exaggerated story, but on the whole, is someone I enjoy spending time with. How does Christina fit into all of this?"

"I got off on a technicality and realised what a lucky escape I'd had. I turned my life around. I even started a community program in my local high school in western Sydney to help teenagers affected by alcohol and drugs. I had a new life and left the old one buried behind me when I moved here." A snarl curled the corner of Daniel's lip. "I was upfront with Christina when I applied for the job at *The Chronicle* and she said that it didn't matter and that I was just the kind of go-getter she was looking for. Little did I know that she would use my past failures against me. It started as a favour here and there, but she was getting more demanding by the day. It was like she wanted me to be at her beck and call twenty hours a day. As if she was the only person in my life. Then I met Suzi at Beth and Lincoln's wedding and we hit it off. I like her, really like her. So I told Christina it was over. I wasn't her puppet anymore"

"And how did she take it?" Clair asked.

Daniel's grave expression said it all. "Not very well, I'm afraid. She wouldn't let up and then only a few days before she was killed, she'd told me that she created her own spin on the story that painted me in a more damning light. She said that unless I dumped Suzi, she was going to plaster my past all over the paper for the whole town to see. She wouldn't tell me where she stored her damning information about me. I couldn't let that happen."

Oh no, what did you do? "But you said you didn't kill Christina?"

His head snapped up. "I didn't. I told Suzi everything and she convinced me that the past is where it should stay. I haven't touched a drop of alcohol ever since that night." His eyes softened as he spoke of Suzi. "She's the most amazing woman I've ever met. She also said people in this town may judge, but they also listen and give people a fair go."

"She's right. Well, for most of us," Cassidy said, remembering her wasted interactions with

Detective Anderson. *He doesn't give you a fair go. Otherwise, he'd believe I was innocent.*

"So why would you print the lies about me in the paper?" Cassidy asked.

"I didn't want to, but Christina was so jealous of you all."

"Jealous," they said in unison.

"Of us?" Cassidy asked.

He nodded. "You see, she wanted the shop that CC's Simply Cupcakes occupies and when the council said you could have it instead of her, she never forgave you for stealing it out from under her. She told me that I was to make you pay and if I didn't, she'd expose me and she'd let nothing stand in her way. She was a very powerful woman."

Cassidy sucked in a deep breath. "I don't believe what I'm hearing. I guess that explains why she wanted to get on the council and when Mayor Windsor said no, she went after him as well. That woman was some piece of work."

"On the night Christina was killed, I wasn't home alone in bed as I originally told you," he said shyly.

"Where were you?"

"An AA meeting. When I moved here, my sponsor was worried that I'd fall back into my old ways, so we agreed that three times a month I would travel back home to attend a meeting with him. It just happened to fall on that night. I left early that morning and drove straight here. You can ask him if you want to."

Cassidy shook her head. While she'd hit another brick wall, she was secretly glad Daniel was innocent, for Suzi's sake. "That's okay, I believe you. I just want you to know that while Ashton Point is a small town and it has its gossip-mongers, on the whole, they're good people. Even if they find out about your past—some may hold it against you—but most, like us, will commend you for turning your life around."

"That's right. And if they don't, they'll have to deal with Cassidy and me," Clair said in her best macho voice.

Tears brimmed the edge of his eyes once more. "Thank you, you don't know how much that means to me."

"Although," Cassidy paused, eyeing Daniel suspiciously once more. "If you print any more information about me without checking with me first, that could be a deal breaker."

Daniel crossed his heart with his finger. "Never again. Promise."

"Then I think we're done, here," she said as she stood followed by Clair. Daniel showed them out, but just before they left he turned and said, "Don't forget, you promised me to keep me in the loop on the big story."

Cassidy sighed. "Don't worry. When we know something concrete, you'll hear about it."

After Daniel had closed the door, she stood on the sidewalk for a moment processing all she'd just heard. "That was pretty intense."

Clair's eyes clouded with sympathy. "You're not wrong. Poor guy."

"I had no idea he'd been through so much. No wonder Suzi has been spending more time with him lately," Cassidy said just as her phone rocked out Bruno Mars' 24K Magic.

"Hello. ...oh my gosh, slow down." Cassidy rolled her eyes.

"Cassidy, are you even listening to me?" Charlotte snapped down the line.

"If you'd slow down and breathe, maybe I would be able to hear you better."

What's going on? Clair mouthed.

"Suzi had to go, her mum's not well and I need help to deliver an order to Margarete over at the Tea 4 Two Café before she closes. I've got about twenty-five minutes and I can't leave this place looking the way it does. Pierre cancelled his trip to Sydney so he'll be in tomorrow and he'll have a conniption if I leave it in this state." Charlotte's frantic voice had Cassidy and Clair in fits of laughter.

"Okay, calm down. I'm actually in town, so I can pop over and pick up the order and drop it off. How does that sound?" Cassidy asked, knowing full well she would be in Charlotte's good books.

"You're a life saver. Okay, I'll get them ready now. See you in a bit. Bye." Charlotte hung up.

Clair smiled and raised an eyebrow. "I'm guessing from that call, you're off to see Charlotte to help deliver her order?"

"Got it in one." Cassidy leant in, giving Clair a quick hug before they headed off in different directions.

Chapter Thirteen

BY THE TIME Cassidy arrived at the Tea 4 Two Café, it was ten minutes before closing, but there were still several customers enjoying Margarete's delicious food. *It never ceases to amaze me how popular this café is.* The one delight they didn't serve was cupcakes, which meant they were no competition for CC's Simply Cupcakes. Not wanting to interrupt, Cassidy placed the boxes of cupcakes on the side counter and waited to catch Margarete's eye. A cold chill scurried up her spine and she shivered as if someone had walked over her grave. *Silly old wives' tale.*

"Oh my gosh, Cassidy, I didn't see you standing there," Margarete said, coming around the counter. She peeked inside one of the boxes and gasped in delight. "They're stunning. You're a lifesaver. I owe you guys big-time. My cousin was supposed to organise the cake for Oma's eightieth

185

birthday dinner tonight but rang in a tizzy, freaking out that she didn't have enough time to get it sorted and dumped it in my lap," Margarete said as she squeezed the air out of Cassidy's lungs in a giant-sized hug. "Thank goodness for Charlotte, I can't believe how she was able to whip up these gorgeous cupcakes in such little time."

The glow in Margarete's eyes sent a bolt of satisfaction through Cassidy. The ability to make someone smile with your own creation hit Cassidy square in the chest, whether it be a newly-designed house or a box of cupcakes. "I'll pass on your appreciation to Charlotte."

"Please do. I've got a little more to do here and there are a few customers still finishing up, but after they've gone I'll give her a call myself and personally thank her," Margarete said returning to the service counter.

"I'm sure she'd love that. Have a great dinner." Cassidy waved goodbye and headed for the door.

"Excuse me. Miss." The stark voice called from the side of the counter.

"Yes?" Cassidy hadn't seen the man around town before. Then again, it was coming into the Christmas season, but he wasn't exactly dressed for the holidays. He was a middle-aged man, sporting a dark, navy, double-breasted suit and fedora. Cassidy's interest was piqued, especially as her eye caught sight of his briefcase on the floor beside him. He pointed to the framed picture on the wall above the corner table. "Is that your local detective?"

Cassidy nodded. "Yes, Detective Anderson. He was a hero that day. He saved young Missy from her house when it went up in flames." She paused and waited for him to continue, but he stood as still as a statue staring at the picture seemingly lost in his own thoughts. "Can I help you with something?" she asked eager to find out his story.

His head snapped around and he smiled, the frown marring his forehead melting away. "Oh, I'm terribly sorry. How rude of me." He pulled a business card out of his coat pocket and handed it to her. "My name is Christopher Linnell."

She took the card and her gaze scanned the classic embossed print. *Christopher Linnell, Attorney.* "Cassidy McCorrson. Are you looking for Detective Anderson?"

His stared at the picture like it would vanish at any second. "I wasn't, but I am now."

"I'm sorry, I'm not following." Cassidy felt like a fish out of water struggling to decipher a riddle.

He chuckled and turned his warm smiling olive-green eyes toward her. "Forgive me. I am, or should I say *was*, Christina Jacobs' lawyer."

Cassidy's eyes widened and she just about fell over. *Of course. How could I forget? It was right here in this very café where Christina had mentioned his name.* "I seem to remember Christina mentioning you. Aren't you some big-time lawyer in Sydney?" Her brow creased. "What are you doing in Ashton Point?"

"I work for the Jacobs family. As you can imagine, they are extremely distressed about their daughter's murder and haven't been able to get any confirmed answers out of the police. They haven't been able to get back from overseas as quickly as they'd hoped. Mrs Jacobs asked me to come up and see if I can expedite the situation."

Distressed? Me too, but for different reasons. Her suspicions grew and she felt her gut knot in two.

His focus returned to the picture. "But now I see my job is going to be harder than I thought."

"You've lost me, I'm afraid," Cassidy said, her nerves on edge.

"That man in the picture isn't who you think he is," he said in a cautious tone.

"He isn't."

He shook his head. "No." He pointed to the empty table under the picture. "Maybe we should sit." Cassidy joined him at the table, her knots doubling in anticipation. "I know this may be hard to believe and I probably shouldn't be telling you this, but the man in that picture is a wanted criminal."

Cassidy felt the blood drain from her cheeks. *What the... He can't be serious?*

"Judging by the look on your face, you had no idea. Your beautiful coastal tourist town is secretly harbouring one of the most wanted men in Australia."

Cassidy swallowed the lump in her throat and she felt as if she'd just been thrown head first into the latest episode of *Underbelly*. This wasn't real, it couldn't be. Things like this don't happen in Ashton Point. Do they?

He took out his notepad and began scribbling notes. "How long ago did Detective Anderson arrive in Ashton Point?"

"Um…my family has only lived here for three years and he's been here for about five before that," Cassidy said in a shaky voice.

"That sounds about right. He disappeared about eight or nine years ago after a major drug bust. He was a major dealer, very high up in the drug syndicate. He was known for bringing drugs into Melbourne on his boat but no-one could ever catch them in his possession. He and his boat were always clean. There was talk of inside connections. That's why he always slipped through the system. He was the best at what he did. Not only did he ship drugs, but he was also known as The Enforcer. When Johnny was sent to deliver a message, you could be sure they knew it came from JBG. The corpses of his victims were always left unrecognisable. His crime scenes weren't exactly for the faint hearted. We could never get the evidence we needed to prosecute, or the witnesses to testify."

Cassidy sat dumbfounded, the new information rolling around in her mind. "Are you sure Anderson is this guy you're talking about? Maybe you could be mistaken?"

He whipped out his phone and started to dial. "No, I'm certain. If what you say is true, the people in this town are in very serious danger. I'm calling it in."

Yeah, me, for starters.

Linnell waited for someone to pick up his call. He sighed, frustrated. "Let me try my other contact," he said, dialling again. He glanced toward the picture while he waited. "He looks different, older and his hair and complexion have changed, but I'd know those eyes anywhere. I've been trying to prosecute him for over fifteen years. His face is ingrained in my memory. I'd never forget those eyes. Sometimes, I can still see the faces of his victims when I go to sleep at night."

While he spoke, Cassidy's gaze scanned the café and the laughing sounds of holidaymakers filled her heart. *Holy cow, none of us are safe.* Her heart clenched as she thought of her sisters in danger…and Finn. Something in Linnell's explanation made her pause. *He was known for bringing drugs into Melbourne on his boat but no-one could ever catch them in his possession.* Anderson had a boat? The story he told about being stung by a jellyfish when he was eight was a complete lie.

The room swayed around her and the continual flow of the final customer's voices pounded her head. She gripped the edge of the table, sucking in a deep breath. "Oh my gosh," she said her frightened gaze locking on to Christopher as he ended his call.

He lied about the boat. Anderson found the money in my room and he was the only one to mention the note. It all adds up to Anderson. "It was Anderson, I mean Johnny. He killed Christina."

His brow creased. "How do you know?"

"It has to be. It all makes sense now. He was here in the café when Christina returned. Christina and I had a kind of disagreement and she said her lawyer would be up at the end of the week. I said some things that I shouldn't have and they could have been interpreted as a threat. He used that against me. Christina said your name and Anderson was here in the café."

He frowned. "She did?"

Cassidy continued, adrenaline coursing through her body. "He knew that if you came to Ashton Point his secret would be out. That you'd discover his identity. So, he got rid of Christina and framed me. Maybe he thought she knew about his past identity, maybe she did. She had an uncanny way of finding the hidden dirt on people and then using it against them. For all he knew, she'd found out before coming back to Ashton Point. Either way, it paints a clear picture of Detective Anderson as the murderer." Her gaze glanced up at the picture. "But he forgot about the picture…or maybe he thought he was safe after he murdered Christina."

"I have people on their way. Now, I suggest you go straight home and tell no-one of our conversation or that I'm in town," Linnell said as he stood.

"Christina wasn't a silly woman. If she knew about Anderson's past she would have had evidence. Blackmail was her speciality." Cassidy said, the cogs in her brain spinning out of control.

"Is there anyone at all at the Ashton Point Police station that you can trust?" Linnell asked.

"Robert," Cassidy said as she stood, her insides in knots. "I've known Robert since I moved here and I trust him."

Linnell nodded and picked up his briefcase ready to leave. "Okay, now, straight home and let me deal with Detective Anderson."

Cassidy drove toward home on autopilot, her mind running over her conversation with Linnell for the hundredth time. *I can't believe Detective Anderson is a mobster and that he killed Christina.* She must have had some major evidence to blackmail him with. The question is, where is that evidence and has Anderson found it already? Maybe Christina still has it, hidden. If she could find it there's no way Anderson would be able to deny his past. A quick detour on the way home couldn't hurt. After all, Linnell said he would take care of Anderson.

Cassidy dialled Finn's number. Two pairs of eyes searching were better than one. *Great, voicemail.* "Finn, it's Cassidy. Detective Anderson is the murderer. Don't ask me how I know, it's a long story, but trust me. He's the one. I'm on my way home and I'll explain everything, but first I'm just making a short detour via Christina's house. I think she was blackmailing him, just as she was Emmerson and

Daniel, and if she was, there has to be evidence somewhere... Call me when you get this message."

Cassidy's hands shook as she drove in the direction of Christina's house. Her body was so tense it was like a volcano ready to erupt any second. She drove down the street, scoping out the scene for anything out of the ordinary before she turned into Christina's driveway. It all appeared calm. Her hands stuck to the steering wheel, excitement worked its way up to her throat from her belly. She sucked in a deep breath and centred herself, pulling Christina's house key from her bag.

Chapter Fourteen

FINN KNOCKED BACK the last drop in his water bottle and grabbed his wallet and keys off the garden bench. "Looks like I might be hanging around Ashton Point for a while longer, so if you need any more help, let me know," he said as he and Liam headed toward the car loaded up with tools.

Liam smirked. "Ah, I thought that might be the case. A cute little red-head caught your attention, has she?"

No use hiding the truth. He chuckled. "I think it was pretty obvious from the start how I felt about Cassidy."

"Yeah and judging by what I walked in on earlier, I think Cassidy's worked it out too," Liam said as he threw his tools in the back of his ute.

A shiver crossed his chest. *She will when I get the time to show her how good it can be between us. Maybe she'd like to do dinner out?* "I'm just gonna give Cass a quick call to see if she wants to grab a bite to eat."

"No worries."

Finn pulled out his phone and saw that it was still on silent from when they'd snuck up on Emmerson. "What the?" he muttered. A missed call and a message from Cassidy. He felt the blood run cold in his veins as he listened to her animated voice. Finn's heart plummeted as he processed her words. Fear for her safety festered deep in his belly. "I don't believe that woman."

Liam paused and frowned. "What's wrong?"

"We need to go. Now," Finn said moving double time to help Liam with the last of the tools.

"What are you talking about? Go where?" Liam asked, unease lacing his words.

"That message was from Cassidy and somehow, she didn't say how, but she's dead set sure Detective Anderson murdered Christina." Liam's eyes widened. "And she's got it into her head that Christina might have been blackmailing him. She's gone back to Christina's house to look for evidence."

"Are you serious?" Liam said starting the engine.

Finn's voice was almost frantic. "I know I'm probably blowing this way out of proportion but the thought of Cassidy snooping around that house alone scares the living daylights out of me." Finn began dialling. First, Cassidy. His heart skipped a beat when it rang out. Maybe she told Clair what happened. Next, he dialled her number and waited.

Liam stepped on the accelerator. "I know the feeling well, she sounds just like her sister. I'm on it. We'll be at Christina's in twenty-five." Liam huffed and shook his head. "What is with McCorrson women and murder? It seems to find them wherever they go."

Everywhere Cassidy looked she came up empty-handed. Frustration dampened her enthusiasm for the search. She hoped Linnell had better luck apprehending Anderson than she had finding the evidence. Christina's house came up empty, and the retreat seems to be heading the same way. "Maybe I was wrong," she muttered, glancing at her watch. "Where are you, Finn? I need help, I can't do this by myself." *Ten more minutes and I'm out of here.*

She mentally crossed off each piece of furniture as she searched it. Coffee table draw, hall cupboard, kitchen dresser. "Nothing." She sighed, closing the last of the sideboard drawers. *Maybe* The Chronicle *might hold more answers.* "Once Linnell nails Anderson to the wall, it won't be my problem anymore. This will be over."

Cassidy spotted her toolbox under the table by the lounge. Last time she and Finn were here with Emmerson, she'd walked out empty handed. "This time I'm taking you with me. This job has cost me enough already." In her haste, she pulled the box out and the latch unclipped itself. The entire contents spilled out onto the Lugano shaggy rug. "Great…that's all I need to put me behind schedule."

The image of her on all fours on the floor flashed in her mind. Not the most elegant position. She was glad Finn hadn't arrived. Embarrassment shot through her as she shuffled on her hands and knees gathering pins, paint swatches, measuring tapes and a photograph. "What is…this?" she whispered as she paused, resting against the white leather couch, her gaze scanning the picture.

The damning image before her stole her breath, her blood froze. *I found it, I can't believe I found it. Thank you, Christina.*

She only knew one man in the picture, but there was no doubt in her mind that it was a younger version of Anderson or Johnny. He stood in the centre of two other men, on the deck of a yacht in the middle of the ocean. Each man was holding a gun. She hadn't a clue where Christina had found it, she was just glad she did. "Gotcha now."

"Got who now?"

Fear ricocheted through her body as she bolted from the ground and came face to face with a cold-blooded murderer. *Detective Anderson.* How had he gotten in without her hearing? Her pulse sped and she slowly eased her hand behind her back. Her fingers began to tingle from gripping the photograph so tightly. "Detective Anderson, what are you doing here? How did you get in?"

He shoved his hands in his pockets. "I'm off duty but had a few loose ends that I couldn't get off my mind. I came through the back door, but I think the more important question is, what are you doing here, and how did you get in?"

"Oh." She paused. "I hadn't had a chance to return the keys. I figured I'd just pop by and pick up my toolbox."

His eyebrows rose. "Did you now?"

She nodded, her mind raced with information overload. *You're looking for the photograph in my hand, aren't you? I was right. Christina* was *blackmailing you and you've come to find and destroy the evidence.* She discreetly lifted the back of her shirt and tucked the photograph into the waistband of her pants. It was up to Cassidy to get this photograph to the police, with or without Finn. A job that was going to prove harder with the murderer standing only meters away.

He glanced past her at the mess on the floor by her toolbox. "I see you found it. What else did you find?"

She frowned praying her voice sounded calm. "What do you mean 'what else?'" Cassidy's heart pounded inside her chest.

Anderson edged his way from the kitchen toward the front door, blocking her closest exit. "I heard you say, 'Gotcha.' Care to elaborate?" His relaxed voice sent shivers up her spine.

No! The word screamed inside her head. She smiled and casually moved toward the kitchen. "I was talking about my toolbox. I found it."

"Come on, Cassidy. I know you better than you think I do. You're hiding something. Out with it. It could help the investigation," he said, the tension in his voice increasing a notch.

Oh, it will definitely help the investigation.

"I have nowhere to be, so I guess we'll be staying here 'til you fess up and I only have so much patience. You can either share with me of your own free will or—"

Fight mode kicked in and Cassidy's mouth ran away from her. "Or what? You'll take matters into your own hands?"

Anderson's face paled. "What did you say?"

Panic bled through her, but it was too late to call back her words now. "I think you heard exactly what I said."

He looked shocked. "You think I'd dish out justice for my own personal gain? Now, why on earth would you think that?"

"So, Christina wasn't blackmailing you? Like she was Emmerson, Daniel, and Mayor Windsor."

He balked at her statement. "I'm a detective. I hardly think I am going to succumb to blackmail."

Finn, where are you? I could use your help right about now. Cassidy kept her feet moving slowly toward the kitchen where she could make a run for it if she could distract him long enough. It was time for the truth to come out.

His eyes darkened and the silence between them was as sharp as a broken piece of glass. She held her breath as Anderson's expression turned sinister and he started to laugh. He opened his arms in surrender. "You got me. Not quite sure how you found out, but kudos to you."

Holy cow. She froze and her feet suddenly felt like lead weights. She hadn't really expected him to confess. "You admit that you killed Christina?"

"Don't be ridiculous. I didn't kill anyone," he said in a spine-chilling tone. "I'm an upstanding member of the Ashton Point community. People are never going to believe I could be capable of murder."

Her pulse kicked up a notch and she felt nauseous at her predicament. Distraction was her best bet at escaping with her life intact.

"Now, Johnny, he's as different from me as cupcakes are to soufflés." He began to pace as he spoke, all the while keeping his eye firmly on Cassidy. "For example, Detective Anderson would probably let you walk out of here. Johnny knows, just as you do, that you'll never see another sunrise."

Cassidy swallowed the lump in her throat. Thoughts of never seeing her sisters and Finn again spurred her to keep fighting. *Keep him talking.* "What happened with Christina? If my life is to end tonight, the least you can do is tell me the whole story."

He paused, then smiled. "Very well. Christina thought she was smart but blackmailing me was her biggest mistake."

Keep him talking. "So, instead of reporting her, you decided to deal with it yourself and pin the blame on me in the process. As you used to do in the old days"

His ominous laugh sent chills right to her core. "If I dealt with her the way I used to, no-one would have recognised her body, let alone been able to identify her."

Cassidy swallowed the bile that pitched itself in her throat. She sucked in a deep breath steadying herself. "So, what happened?"

"Christina had to go and get the same stupid lawyer that's been trying to crucify me for the past nine years. Good old Christopher Linnell. You heard her in the café, he was coming up at the end of the week. No reason for the lawyer to visit Ashton Point if there was no Christina."

Too late. "Why blame it on me?"

"That was the easy part. I couldn't believe my luck when you two started your petty bickering. Between the threats flying back and forth and the money she owed you, the pieces just fell into place."

Anger slowly began to gnaw at her chest. "You planted the money in my room and wrote the note, didn't you?"

He made a fake bow which angered her even more. "Guilty as charged. You have to admit, it was genius. You were the perfect scapegoat. After all, three murders have been blamed on McCorrson women. What's one more?"

One too many. Cassidy stiffened as Anderson edged his way toward her.

"Now, my only quandary is how to get rid of you. Being off duty, I don't have my gun with me, but then again, I wouldn't want the bullet traced back to me. There's the old-fashioned way or I could make it look like another break-in gone wrong?"

She barely had time to turn and run before he lunged for her, grabbing her hair, jerking her head backwards. She hit the carpet with a thud, jolting the air out of her lungs. Terrified, her heart stopped as he came at her again. Cassidy's head swam. She had two choices, live or die. There was only one outcome she was prepared to settle for.

Just as he reached for her, she brought her knee up and slammed it into his groin with the full force of a champion boxer's punch. He fell to the ground gasping for air. The sudden echo of sirens in the distance spurred her on. She rolled on the ground, fumbling toward the door, her escape in sight. He dove for her ankle, dragging her back down toward him.

"You're going to pay for that. Come here."

"Get off me," she screamed, her voice stricken with fear. She kicked and screamed as hard as she could until her gaze caught sight of her level, semi-hidden under the couch. The louder sirens confirmed they were getting closer. *Oh, please hurry.* Her shaky hand encircled the icy metal object and she closed her eyes and swung it as hard as she could toward Anderson.

"Ahhhh," he shrieked, releasing her ankle. Adrenaline flooded her as she bolted for the door.

A blur of activity surrounded her and she turned in time to hear Robert yell, "Freeze." His gun was pointed directly at Anderson's chest. "Don't move a single muscle. You're under arrest for the murder of Christina Jacobs." In seconds, several police officers surrounded Anderson and it was finally over.

Finn's hands ran over her body frantically. "Cassidy, are you all right? Did he hurt you? Do you need to go to the hospital?"

Cassidy gripped Finn's shoulders for support, her wobbly legs doing their darndest to hold her up. She barely had time to catch her breath before her entire family, boyfriends included, and Christopher Linnell stormed through the door. "No, I'm okay. I'm a bit shaken up and I'll be stiff for a few days."

"I told you all to wait outside," Robert snapped at them as he watched Kayne cuff Anderson.

Charlotte turned on Robert, daggers shooting from her eyes. "Robert Loughlin, if you think I'm going to wait outside while my sister is in danger, then you're sadly mistaken. I think we have proven McCorrson women can take care of themselves."

Robert shook his head and rolled his eyes upward as Christopher Linnell stepped forward. The air thickened. "Well, well, well. We finally meet hey, Johnny."

"I don't know who you are or what you're talking about. You've got nothing on me," Anderson snarled.

"Actually, we have," Cassidy said, pulling the photograph out of the waistband of her pants and handing it to Linnell. Anderson paled. His gaze shot from Cassidy to the photograph and back again. "I think this is what got Christina killed. A picture of our sweet detective here in his past life."

Linnell scanned the picture and a smile worked its way across his face. "You're one very lucky young lady." He held up the picture. "Thank you. This is going to put Johnny away for a long, long time."

"Good," Cassidy said. "While Christina wasn't always the nicest person, no-one deserves to die such a horrible death. Please pass on my condolences to her parents when you speak with them."

"I will. Thank you." He turned and left leaving her sisters to fuss over her.

She turned to face them. "I guess we won't be needing Caroline's help after all."

They all responded at the same time and it was like listening to the gibberish Olympics. "Okay, stop, please. This isn't helping my head one iota."

"Oh gosh, sorry. But you had us scared to death," Clair said encasing her in a hug. "Finn called and told us about your message. I just thank goodness we got here in time."

Me too. There were mumbles of agreement from all. "Cassidy, I think you know the drill. You'll need to come into the station and give a statement."

"Tonight?" Finn asked.

"Yes, tonight. The sooner, the better," Robert said as he started shooing everyone outside. "This is now a crime scene, so I am going to have to ask you all to step outside."

They gathered on the front lawn. "Do you want us to take you to the station?" Charlotte asked.

"That won't be necessary," Finn said, snaking his arm around Cassidy's waist. "I can take her, if that's okay with you, Liam? I'm not letting her out of my sight again."

Cassidy caught the suspicious glances between Charlotte and Clair.

Liam handed over his keys to Finn. "Sure. I'll grab a lift with Clair."

"Does that mean we can expect to see you around town a while longer?" Clair asked sheepishly.

Finn tilted his head to the side. "That all depends on Cassidy."

Cassidy's chest hurt and she was about to fall where she stood, but she refused to succumb to her fatigued body until she knew what Finn meant by his comment. "Thank you for coming, but I'm okay. You all should head home and then after I finish at the police station, Finn will bring me home."

"Are you sure?" She nodded and they all hugged and she watched them as they headed to their vehicles.

Finn turned, his eyes full of anguish. "You have no idea what it did to me tonight when I listened to your message. Then when I rang Clair, Linnell was there and she told me what he'd said and all I could think about was that I might never see you again."

Cassidy cringed at the heartache she'd caused him. "I'm sorry, I didn't mean to scare you."

He stepped closer and pushed a strand of hair behind her ear. His lips were so close she could almost taste them. "I was scared because I thought I might never be able to tell you that I want to stay in Ashton Point with you. I don't know if what I feel in my heart is love, but I know that I don't want to live without you."

Love? Oh my! Her gaze fell to his lips as they descended on hers. She floated and the pain and exhaustion that plagued her body fell away as if it had been washed down a stream. He pulled her closer and she snaked her arms around his neck wanting more.

He finally ended the kiss but kept his arms tight around her. Resting his forehead on hers, he said, "I suppose I should get you to the station."

Contentment filled her heart. "Mmmm."

"So, tell me. Is life in Ashton Point going to always be this eventful?" he asked.

"Oh, no."

"That's good. I don't think my heart would be able to take any more nights like tonight." He pulled his arms tight around her.

She giggled and snuggled closer. "I promise, it's going to be way more exciting." Finn had brought love and happiness back into her life. No more deceit and heartache, no more loneliness. Her life was finally heading in the right direction. As long as she stayed on the right side of the law, what more could she ask for?

The End

Thank you for reading **Cupcakes and Corpses**

If you enjoyed this story, I would really appreciate it if you would consider leaving a review of this book, no matter how short, at the retailer site where you bought your copy or on sites like Amazon or Goodreads.

YOU are the key to this book's success and the success of **The Cupcake Capers Cozy Mystery Series.** I read every review and they really do make a huge difference.

Keep up to date on Polly's book releases, signings and events on her website:
https://www.pollyholmesmysteries.com
Join Polly's Official Facebook Reader Group:
Danger, Mystery and Romance with Hint of Cozy Sweetness.
https://www.facebook.com/groups/217817788798223

About the Author

Polly Holmes is the cheeky, sassy alter ego of Amazon best-selling author, P.L. Harris. When she's not writing her next romantic suspense novel as P.L. Harris, she is planning the next murder in one of Polly's cozy mysteries.

According to Polly, the best part about writing cozy mysteries is researching. Finding the best way to hook the reader, a great way to murder someone, a plethora of suspects and of course a good dose of sweet treats thrown in for good measure.

Polly lives not far from the beach in the northern suburbs of Perth, Western Australia with her Bishion Frise, Bella. When she's not writing you can find her sipping coffee in her favourite cafe, watching reruns of Murder, She Wrote or taking long walks along the beach soaking up the fresh salty air.

You can visit *Polly Holmes* at her website: www.pollyholmesmysteries.com or follow her on her Official Facebook Reader Group: Danger, Mystery and Romance with a hint of Cozy Sweetness. https://www.facebook.com/groups/217817788798 223

Check out the complete Cupcake Capers Series

Book 1 – Cupcakes and Cyanide

Book 2 – Cupcakes and Curses

Book 3 – Cupcakes and Corpses

Book 4 – Murder and Mistletoe

Cupcakes and Cyanide

**Welcome to Ashton Point. One sweet taste
could be her last.**

Charlotte McCorrson has spent her entire life
building her business, CC's Simply Cupcakes. The town of
Ashton Point is her home and she's garnered a reputation
of stellar service and delightful pastries, one nibble at a
time. But everything isn't as sweet in the sleepy, coastal
town as Charlotte would like to think. She is in for a rude
awakening and no amount of sugar will make this
medicine go down any smoother.

After catering a large town-wide event, Ashton
Point's morning newspaper fills Charlotte McCorrson
with an icy sense of dread. The headlines scream *Cupcake
Killer!* and put the blame squarely on CC's Simply
Cupcakes. When bodies begin to pile up behind her
confectionary goodies, Charlotte must prove that while
her cupcakes are delicious, they aren't literally to die for—
before she ends up in jail for a crime she didn't commit.

This is Book 1 in The Cupcake Capers Series and
may contain elements of humour, drama and danger.
However, it will definitely not contain any of the following
potentially lethal substances:

Swearing or profanity.

Gore or graphic scenes.

Cliff-hangers or unsolved endings.

Cupcakes and Curses

When it comes to design, death is in the details.

Cassidy McCorrson has worked hard to develop her reputation as a leading interior designer in her seaside town of Ashton Point. Since arriving home from visiting her parents in New York, her skills have been in high demand. Between juggling the design for her sister's new cupcake shop and her private client, Cassidy barely has time to prepare for the upcoming Christmas celebrations.

Cassidy is excited at the prospect of delivering designs she can be proud of, but her world is turned upside down when the body of a local reporter is found murdered on location at her latest work site. What should have been a straightforward job turns out to be the worst decision of her life.

In order to clear her name and restore her reputation, Cassidy must find the real killer before she ends up redesigning the interior of a jail cell. Can she unearth the killer before time runs out?

This is Book 2 in The Cupcake Capers Series and may contain elements of humour, drama and danger. However, it will definitely not contain any of the following potentially lethal substances:

Swearing or profanity.

Gore or graphic scenes.

Cliff-hangers or unsolved endings.

Cupcakes and Corpses

When it comes to design, death is in the details.

Cassidy McCorrson has worked hard to develop her reputation as a leading interior designer in her seaside town of Ashton Point. Since arriving home from visiting her parents in New York, her skills have been in high demand. Between juggling the design for her sister's new cupcake shop and her private client, Cassidy barely has time to prepare for the upcoming Christmas celebrations.

Cassidy is excited at the prospect of delivering designs she can be proud of, but her world is turned upside down when the body of a local reporter is found murdered on location at her latest work site. What should have been a straightforward job turns out to be the worst decision of her life.

In order to clear her name and restore her reputation, Cassidy must find the real killer before she ends up redesigning the interior of a jail cell. Can she unearth the killer before time runs out?

This is Book 3 in The Cupcake Capers Series and may contain elements of humour, drama and danger. However, it will definitely not contain any of the following potentially lethal substances:

Swearing or profanity.
Gore or graphic scenes.
Cliff-hangers or unsolved endings.

Mistletoe and Murder

Mistletoe magic or the kiss of death?

Alexandra Cohen is determined to show her boss she has what it takes to be manager of The Springs Café on the outskirts of Ashton Point. She's smart and with the addition of CC's Simply Cupcakes, sales have sky-rocketed. The town is in full holiday spirit and with the Christmas Fair fast approaching, Alex has to work twice as hard to keep her interfering ex-boyfriend, out of the picture before he destroys her life forever.

After reluctantly agreeing to run the kissing booth at the fair, Alex has to deal with a continuous line of male customers, as well as an ex who has ignored her requests to leave her alone. But the day is really tarnished when Alex stumbles across a body on the ground of her kissing booth dressed as Santa.

The evidence is gathering against her and Alex must decide if she should let the police do their job and pray they do it well or if she should take matters into her own hands. With the help of the McCorrson sisters, Alex must investigate so she doesn't become the town scapegoat and forced to spend Christmas behind bars.

This is Book 4 in The Cupcake Capers Series and may contain elements of humour, drama and danger. However, it will definitely not contain any of the following potentially lethal substances:

Swearing or profanity.

Gore or graphic scenes.

Cliff-hangers or unsolved endings.

Read on for and excerpt of Cupcakes and Cyanide

Charlotte's Story

Chapter One

"CALLING ALL THE single ladies." Charlotte McCorrson stood nestled at the back of the reception centre, semi-hidden behind a burgundy-and-white, balloon topiary tree.

Great. Bouquet throwing time, just what I need. For every man in the room to know I'm still single. When Beth invited her to the wedding she was over the moon, after all, they'd been good friends since Clair and her family moved to Ashton Point three years ago. What she hadn't planned on was still being single by the time the wedding rolled around.

They may as well take out a front-page ad in the Ashton Point Chronicle. She could see it now. "Ashton Point master cupcake baker extraordinaire struggles to snag herself a husband. Could she be lacking that special ingredient all men are looking for? What is wrong with the redheaded beauty?" She'd been over the moon when Beth and Lincoln asked CC's Simply Cupcakes to design a wedding cake, based around Charlotte's award-winning cupcake designs.

"Charlotte? What are you doing back here?" A petite voice spoke from behind.

She spun, her breath catching as her gaze landed on a vision in white. Decked out in a satin Karen Willis Holmes, floor-length, empire dress with embroidered tulle overlay, Beth looked like an angel. There had barely been a dry eye in the church as she walked down the aisle to her handsome prince. The fairy-tale wedding every bride dreams of.

Charlotte stiffened as Beth threw her arms around her neck and squeezed. "I never got a chance to properly thank you for the wonderful cupcake display you made. It was truly the cake of my dreams. I'm so glad you were able to share my special day with me. It wouldn't have been the same without you and Clair here," she said with a beaming smile.

"You're welcome, I wouldn't have missed it for the world. I'm so happy you liked it," she said in a muffled voice. Her mouth was half covered by blonde ruffles of hair, leaving the metallic taste of hairspray on her tongue.

Beth pulled back and their gazes held strong. "Liked it? Are you serious? I loved it." A bolt of electric energy ran up Charlotte's spine. She cherished the buzz she got from seeing the joy her cupcakes brought others. "And if anyone thinks they're taking the leftovers home tonight, they have another thing coming. That's all I'll be eating 'til we leave for our honeymoon next week."

Both ladies burst into laughter. Beth's happiness was starting to rub off on Charlotte.

"Didn't you hear the MC? You need to get to the dance floor. I'm about to throw the bouquet."

Charlotte cringed at the thought. "No, no, it's fine. I'm really okay sitting back and letting someone else take the limelight." She had planned on falling madly in love with the man of her dreams by the wedding. *I guess life doesn't always go to plan.*

A sliver of disappointment marred Beth's expression. "I can't believe what I'm hearing. Your grandma would be turning in her grave if she knew you were skipping the bouquet toss. You know how she loved tradition."

Warmth filled Charlotte's heart. Her grandmother treasured her independence. She was the reason they'd moved to Ashton Point in the first place.

She shook her head. "I'm happy watching from the sidelines, besides, a mosh pit of single women jumping around like clucking chickens, all vying for their piece of the elusive dream isn't really my idea of fun."

"Now, that's something I'd like to see." A gruff voice echoed in her ear.

"Excuse me?" Charlotte said, spinning to see Lincoln's best man grinning like the Cheshire Cat.

"A mosh pit of single women jumping around like clucking chickens," he said with a cheeky grin. "Definitely something I'd pay money to see."

Beth sighed, rolled her eyes and play-punched him in the shoulder. "Give it a rest, Liam."

Liam… Mmmm. Why is it that all men named Liam are gorgeous? Liam Hemsworth, Liam Neeson. Tanned, tall and handsome, he flashed a half smile at Charlotte and she felt a spike of interest spark in her belly.

Her gaze caught her sister, Clair, waving frantically behind Liam. *Saved by the bell.* "I'm sorry, Beth, but it looks like Clair needs me."

"Charlotte, there you are. I've been looking for you everywhere," Clair said as she joined them, flicking her deep-red ponytail over her shoulder.

"Why, is something wrong?" Alarm hit Charlotte square in the chest. "Please don't tell me we've run out of cupcakes? There should be plenty to go around. I made loads of extras."

Beth folded her arms across her chest and frowned. "Yes, don't tell me we ran out, otherwise the Bridezilla I've kept hidden inside might have to make a guest appearance."

"Bridezilla?" Liam said with a raised eyebrow. "I find that very hard to believe."

"When it comes to Charlotte's cupcakes, you better believe it," she snapped, holding his stern gaze in hers.

"Everyone calm down, there are plenty of cupcakes." Clair smiled and looped her arm through her sisters. "I was looking for Charlotte for the bouquet toss. Nothing better than a little competition between sisters."

A grin spread across Beth's face and she clapped her hands together. "Wonderful. I best go and get ready. Good luck." Beth said as she hurried off.

"This should be a sight to see. I'll let you two ladies get ready. I'd hate to be the one to keep you from your spot in the chicken brood," Liam said with a smile as he strode back to the bridal table at the top of the dance floor.

Clair raised an eyebrow. "Chicken brood?"

"Never mind," Charlotte said, shaking her head.

"Wasn't that the best man?" Clair asked, forcefully guiding Charlotte toward the crowded dance floor.

Charlotte nodded. *Certainly was THE best man.* She let her eyes wander over his retreating figure. Her gaze seemed to have a mind of its own. It made its way down his broad shoulders, to his trim waist and tight derriere. She felt her cheeks grow hot as she imagined what he would look like out of his suit.

"What was his name again?" Clair's words were met with silence. "Earth to Charlotte," she said, flicking Charlotte's forehead as if she were flicking a fly from the back of her hand. "What is his name?" she snapped.

"Oww." Charlotte rubbed her forehead. "All right. I heard you the first time. Liam. His name is Liam."

Charlotte's stomach tightened as Clair elbowed their way to the centre of the dance floor dragging her along for the ride.

"Okay, ladies. Are we ready for the bouquet toss?" The deep, throaty voice of the MC blared out across the room.

Charlotte's body tensed as ear-splitting screams of single women pierced the air. *Oh my, could this be any more embarrassing?*

To top it off, Beyoncé's *Single Ladies* boomed out as Beth took centre stage.

Her breath caught in her throat as her gaze snared Liam's sly grin from the front of the room. *What's with the grin?* Cheers erupted around her and her eyes widened as Beth's bouquet flew straight into her arms.

Charlotte stood in the kitchen, her lungs void of air as the newspaper headline screamed at her like an unwanted nightmare. She held the morning newspaper in her icy fingers. *Cupcake Killer!*

Beth's wedding had been the event of the year, a perfect place to show off her culinary skills. The whole town had turned up to see her finally tie the knot with Lincoln Wade, Ashton Point's most eligible bachelor. Everyone who's anyone had been there, which meant more advertising for their business, CC's Simply Cupcakes.

"I don't believe this." Her hands shook as she read the front-page article. Definitely not the front page she had imagined last night at the wedding. "Why would they think *my* cupcakes killed someone?"

Her eyes were glued to the quote at the bottom of the page next to her picture. *Doctor says two beloved local councilmen are in critical condition and show signs of cyanide poisoning.*

"Cyanide poisoning?" she asked, collapsing on the kitchen stool as her knees gave way. "I do *not* cook with cyanide."

She continued to read. *Guests say that they began feeling ill after the cake was cut and cupcakes distributed.*

"Definitely not from my cupcakes." Anger simmered in her veins. It was going to hit the fan, so to speak, when her sister, Clair, heard of this debacle. Thankfully Cassidy was over visiting Mum and Dad in New York for the next two weeks. At least she won't be tarnished by this nightmare.

This town was their home. They'd moved to Ashton Point on the central coast of New South Wales, just over three years ago to help her grandma. "As if anyone would think I would intentionally poison someone. This is totally unfair," she said, slamming the paper down on the breakfast bar. Her stomach bottoming out as her gaze spotted the bouquet on the kitchen bench.

Clair's weary voice made Charlotte's breath catch in her throat. "What's unfair?" she asked, as she entered the kitchen.

Charlotte's chest tightened like it was being forcibly crushed in a vice. *Damn it, there's no hiding this now.* She scooped up the newspaper before Clair spotted the disaster that was about to tear their dreams apart.

"What's unfair?" Clair repeated heading toward the Nespresso machine and wiping the crusty sleep remnants from the inner rim of her eyes.

Charlotte's pulse sped up. Clearing her throat, she stood and held the newspaper close to her chest, ready to face the music head-on. "I've something to show you, but maybe you should get a coffee and sit down first." Clair was like a five-foot-five, grumpy bed monster with a toothache before her morning coffee.

"For goodness sake, Charlotte, spit it out," she said running her hand through her knotted hair. "I didn't exactly get much sleep last night, by the time we packed up after the wedding."

Charlotte cringed at the mention of the wedding. "You're going to hear about it one way or another." She sighed. "May as well be before you leave the house."

Suspicion worked its way across Clair's face. Leaning against the counter, she folded her arms across her chest. "Okay, enough with the cryptic clues and just tell me what you're talking about."

Charlotte's heart plummeted to the base of her gut. She flipped the paper around and held her breath. Waiting for the incoming explosion.

"Cupcake killer!" Clair's amused, bubbly giggle shot through Charlotte like a dagger. "That's ridiculous. We've known Daniel for three years and everyone in town knows he's big on sensationalising stories without getting his facts straight first. You're not taking that seriously, are you?"

"Of course I'm taking it seriously."

"It's just Daniel trying to big note his career. You and I know there's no truth to it and I'm sure when the truth is revealed, Daniel will be eating his own words." Clair busied herself working her mass of deep-red, bushy hair into a messy bun on the top of her head. "I'm sure it will blow over once they've worked out how they were really poisoned."

Shock bolted through Charlotte's body. "I can't believe you're being so blasé about this. We've worked our butts off to make CC's Simply Cupcakes the best it can possibly be and…" She paused, fury running through her veins. She shook the newspaper in front of Clair's unimpressed expression. "…bad publicity is the last thing we need." Charlotte's stomach grumbled as the fresh scent of roasted hazelnut assaulted her nostrils.

Clair made two fresh cups and handed one off to Charlotte. "Okay, I suppose this isn't ideal, but I'd hardly think one article in the local rag is going to destroy our business. Besides, the whole town knows Daniel will bend the truth to sell one more newspaper."

Clair skimmed over the article. A myriad of emotions flashing across Clair's face made it impossible for Charlotte to determine her thoughts. "They say that no accusations will be acted upon until they have concrete evidence and they'll be following up all leads. Maybe we should keep our eyes and ears open, just in case."

Anxiety crept into Charlotte's mind and compounded her sudden headache into a dull roar. "I agree, but…"

Clair continued, oblivious to Charlotte's annoyance. "And we have Mrs Stevenson's eightieth birthday high tea tomorrow afternoon, down by the river. I'm sure after that goes off without a hitch, Daniel will not only be eating his words, but also your delicious cupcakes."

"Maybe you're right, but I don't think we should wait for the fall out from this article. I know Beth was taking the leftovers home and I don't want her to worry, so I'm going to head over to reassure them that my cupcakes were not the source of the poisoning."

Clair fake coughed. "The morning after their wedding?"

Frustration bubbled up, sending Charlotte's pulse racing. Again. "They're not leaving for their honeymoon 'til Wednesday, and if I remember rightly, Lincoln has to work today to tie up loose ends before they leave."

She glanced one last time at the newspaper and huffed. *This is the most ludicrous thing ever put in print. I'll make you eat your words if it's the last thing I do.*

Clair sighed. "Okay, but don't take too long. I'll be heading over to the shop soon to update the books and make sure we have enough supplies for Mrs Stevenson's order. I'll see you when you get there."

"Okay." Inside, she was furious at Clair's nonchalant attitude. "Mark my words, I'll get to the bottom of this."

Annoyed at the incessant interruption to his morning breakfast, Liam Bradly strutted toward the door. A continuous thunderous roar hammered his head, thanks to his addiction to good wine. He'd stupidly over-indulged at the wedding and his queasy stomach was a stark reminder of why he usually drank red instead of white wine.

He ran his hand through his hair and glanced at the wall clock. "Are you serious?" It's not even nine o'clock yet. Who the hell visits this early on a Saturday morning, especially after a late wedding reception the night before? He'd tear strips off whatever idiot was on the other side of the door.

Liam threw the oak door wide open. "Do you have any idea what time…" He froze mid-sentence, his eyes glued to the petite woman standing before him. He'd remember her anywhere. As if he'd forget a woman of her beauty. Her wavy red locks hung just below her shoulders, framing her face. This was much better than the semi-business look she'd worn yesterday at the wedding, hair pulled back in a tight bun. Now, she was the picture of a woman that would tantalise any man, including him.

She's beautiful.

A soft smile curved her lips, but her eyes told a different story. The drumming in his head shot his mind back to the present. He smiled. "Well, well, if it isn't the Cupcake Killer in person."

She gasped. "You read it too?"

He nodded. "I'm sure everyone in town's read it. Hard not to see it. It was plastered all over the front page."

Her glossy, sapphire-blue eyes widened. Thrusting her hands on her hips she said, "That article is utter nonsense. They had no right to print that without any evidence. My cupcakes were not the reason those people got sick."

"Really?" he asked folding his arms across his chest and giving her an uninterrupted view of his taut biceps and clenched abs.

Her jaw dropped to speak, but nothing came out. The only indication that she was still breathing was the warm, crimson blush that had worked its way from her neck to her cheeks.

"I...um... I wanted to...um..." She bit her bottom lip and paused mid-sentence as if her voice had suddenly vanished.

What the hell is with her eyes? Their constant flittering movement, combined with his throbbing head, was making him nauseous. It was as if she didn't know where to look.

He was standing there in only his pyjama bottoms with the door wide open for the whole neighbourhood to see. A rush of triumph surged through his system. *Nice to know my body can still affect a woman that way.*

He gestured toward his lack of attire. "My apologies, I wasn't expecting visitors," he said as he waved her inside. "Come in while I get something more appropriate on."

She shook her head. "I'm fine. I just wanted to speak to Beth, if she was around."

Liam turned and headed back inside. "Happy to chat after I get dressed. Close the door after you come in will you?"

He hurriedly dressed and walked into the kitchen, half expecting her not to be there. But there she was, standing in front of the sliding glass door framed by the morning glow of the sun. She looked naturally beautiful in a quiet, understated way.

He shoved his hands in his trouser pockets. "Don't tell me... you've decided to cook me breakfast. I'm not sure my stomach can handle one of your delicious cyanide cupcakes this morning."

She spun and stared straight through him. It unnerved him. Colour leached from her face, leaving her white as a sheet. Stepping back, she stumbled.

Liam let out a string of curses as he lunged for her before she face-planted on the kitchen tiles.

"I'm sorry. That was meant to be a joke. Obviously in poor taste," he said, still holding her elbow and refusing to let go until he was sure she had both feet planted firmly on the ground. Liam rubbed the elbow he'd grabbed, trying to alleviate any discomfort he may have caused by his firm grip.

"Yes, poor taste, indeed," she said huskily, easing her arm from his hold.

"It seems we were both rather busy at the wedding yesterday, and after your triumph in the bouquet toss, you disappeared. We never got the chance to formally meet." He held his hand out, eager for the introduction. "I'm Liam Bradly."

She looked at him in bewilderment, as if he were speaking gibberish, then stepped back and thrust her hand out in his direction, clearly determined to keep him at arms-length. "Charlotte McCorrson."

He smiled and shook her hand. "Nice to meet you, Charlotte." His hand pulsed under her warm touch. A soft smile curved her lips, her eyes glittering under the morning sun.

She withdrew her hand from his grip. "I didn't know you were staying here. I actually came over to see Beth. I wanted to reassure her my cakes were not the source of the poisoning and that article is utter garbage."

"Well, as you can see she's not here, or Lincoln for that matter. They left for their honeymoon in the early hours of this morning, but I'm sure they wouldn't believe it anyway."

"Oh," she said anxiously. "I thought they weren't leaving 'til Wednesday?"

"My surprise wedding gift," Liam said. It was the least he could do for his best friend.

"Are you house-sitting for them?" Her eyebrows went up in question.

House-sitting? The thought would have most certainly filled him with dread. That was before he met Charlotte. Now the idea had merit. *I have holidays due, and Lincoln did say to make myself at home before they left.* A week relaxing in this quiet town, getting to know the locals, one in particular, was definitely preferable to heading back to Perth to his mundane job of counting numbers on people's tax returns.

"Yes, I'll be house-sitting while they're on their honeymoon. Maybe you can show me around town while I'm here," he said flashing his cheekiest smile.

She gave him a peculiar look, apprehension entering her gaze. She shook her head. "I'm sorry, I can't. I have to get to the bottom of this poisoning before my entire business is ruined."

"Why would someone want to ruin your business?" he pried.

Annoyance washed over her expression. "As if I would know. It's not like we have enemies in town. I'm sure it's all a big misunderstanding."

He was up for an adventure. "Maybe we could make a deal. You show me around town and I'll help you solve the mystery of the cyanide bandit, what do you say?"

Charlotte froze, panic firing her eyes. She hastily moved past him and headed for the door. "I'm sorry, I can't. Enjoy your stay in Ashton Point."

Her rejection felt like a punch to the stomach. By the time he got his thoughts together, she was gone. "What the hell just happened?"

Chapter Two

"WHAT IS WITH you today?" Clair asked as she pulled the car into St. Edwards Point car park. "You've been like a grumpy teddy bear with a thorn stuck in its side since you arrived at the shop yesterday."

Well, you would be too if your mind was clouded with bulging biceps and washboard abs. Charlotte couldn't very well tell her sister that. Frustration simmered, and she felt her chest tighten as the lie rolled off her tongue. "Sorry, my mind's been preoccupied with this cyanide fiasco, that's all."

You're so full of crap, it's a wonder she doesn't call your bluff.

Every time she remembered her visit to Beth's she made another baking mistake. Thoughts of Liam standing there in only his pyjama bottoms scrambled her brain cells. So, he was cute, big deal. He'd flown in for the wedding, it's not like he'd be staying around for long. In the end, Charlotte had remade a total of thirty-five cupcakes. She was lucky Clair had brought extra ingredients.

Clair huffed and threw Charlotte an annoyed glare as she started unpacking Mrs Stevenson's cupcake order from the back of the car. "It would be nice if you would get your head in the game and focus on the job. We need to get these over to the cake table before the guests arrive."

Focus ... Focus. "Yeah, of course." Pride flooded her heart. She'd taken extra special care to create something spectacular to celebrate Mrs Stevenson's eightieth birthday. "Okay, I can't pick another box up so I'll pop back for the last few once I've delivered these," she said to Clair as she bumped the car door closed with her backside.

"No problem, I'll meet you over there," Clair said and moved off.

Charlotte turned to follow Clair's lead and froze. She blinked several times, positive her eyes were playing tricks on her. *It can't be... no, no, no, it can't be. It is.* Her cheeks flushed, sending a fiery blush roaring up her face until it felt like she'd stuck her head in a blazing oven.

Mr Washboard Abs himself was walking toward her, his eyes boring right through her. What kind of pun was he going to throw her way today? *This is ridiculous. The last thing I need is to be distracted by a man, especially one who is just passing through town, when my whole livelihood is at stake.* She'd had her fair share of failed romances and she wasn't looking to add another to the growing list.

He smiled and shoved his hands in his pockets. "Charlotte, what a nice surprise."

She blinked a few times and her brow creased, puzzled by his appearance. "What on earth are you doing here?" she asked as she manoeuvred past him toward the cake table. "I thought you would have better things to do than attend the eightieth birthday high tea for a lady you've never met." Her words were laced with sarcasm.

He hastily followed on her heels, staying an unnerving foot from her at all times. "You have a point, but the more I thought about my behaviour yesterday, the more annoyed I got with myself. I couldn't leave it a moment longer without apologising to you one more time. I asked around and they told me this is where I'd find you. So"—he shrugged his shoulders—"here I am."

Unease skittered up her spine. He'd sought *her* out?

Approaching the cake table, Clair's voice interrupted her thoughts. "Aren't you going to introduce me to your friend, Charlotte?" Clair said with a smirk as she started unpacking the cakes from Charlotte's boxes.

Charlotte glared at Clair. Since when had he become *her* friend? "Um," she said as she pitched in and helped set up the display. "This is Liam Bradly. Remember, he was the best man at the wedding? He's going to be house-sitting for them while they're on their honeymoon."

"Nice to meet you, Liam Bradly. Do you mind holding these empty boxes a moment?" she said thrusting box after box in his direction.

"Sure."

Charlotte's eyes closed for a brief moment and she squared her shoulders. "Thank you for your help, Liam," she said taking the boxes from his hands. "But I can take it from here." Turning to Clair, she continued. "I'll pop these back and grab the last few boxes."

She was headed for the car before either could return a comment. *Well, that was awkward.* She was only meters from the car when Liam fell into step behind her. She rolled her eyes and kept walking. "Liam, what is it you want?"

"I told you."

She spun and pulled back, his taut body almost bowling her over. He caught her by the arms and she was besieged with sudden awareness.

"I'm sorry, I didn't mean to startle you," he said his tone one of sincerity.

She swallowed the lump in her throat and eased her arms from his grip. "Thank you for apologising again but it really isn't necessary. I have my hands full at the moment with everything that is going on with the shop. I'm not looking to get involved with anyone right now."

He held his hands up to halt her mid-thought. "Woah, slow down. I'm in town for a week at the most. I only came to apologise for being a loud-mouth idiot yesterday. Who said anything about getting involved?"

Charlotte's eyes widened. Her stomach bottomed out and the bitter taste of bile rose to the back of her throat. *Can I put my foot in my mouth any further?* His rejection hurt, but then again, she had a knack for jumping to conclusions.

"Oh."

"I am truly sorry for the pathetic joke I pulled yesterday about your cupcakes and just to prove it, I'd love to taste one." His smile was like a release of fresh air.

What's the harm in being friends? She could do friends.

"Sure, why not," she said putting the empty boxes in the car and replacing them with the last of the full ones. "Let's get these over so Clair doesn't have a freakout. Then I'm sure I'll be able to steal one for you. Just don't tell my sister."

He whispered. "I promise." He thinned his lips and made a locking action with a key and threw it over his shoulder.

A hearty laugh erupted from the base of her stomach. "Come with me."
Liam stood to the side of the table while Charlotte placed the last of the decorations around the cupcake display and then stood back, her heart brimming with satisfaction. *I do love my job.*

"Oh, Charlotte, it's wonderful," Mrs Stevenson said, her eyes bursting with love. She clasped her hands together over her heart. "It's perfect, just as I imagined. You've taken me back to my teenage years dear when high tea was all the fashion."

Adrenaline bled through Charlotte's veins. The love in her eyes was all she needed to pep her spirits up after the disastrous start to the weekend.

"I'm so happy you approve," she said with a smile.

Charlotte's breath caught in her throat as Mrs Stevenson grabbed her in a motherly hug. She couldn't help the surge of longing or sudden tears that burned her eyelids. She'd missed her mum so much since her parents moved to New York a year ago. Her mother was an award-winning interior designer and she spent most of her time travelling between New York and Australia. It'd nearly broken her mother's heart to leave her girls behind, but they'd convinced her it was the best decision for her career. Charlotte missed her terribly, but thanks to Mrs Stevenson's hugs, she felt her mother in her heart. Always.

She blinked back her tears as Mrs Stevenson's voice warmed her heart. "That nonsense written in the paper yesterday was utter codswallop. As far as I'm concerned, you make the best cupcakes I've ever tasted and if I had my way, Daniel would have his backside tanned so hard he couldn't sit down for a week."

Charlotte bit her lip containing a giggle that wanted to escape.

"I couldn't agree more," Liam said, startling her.

Mrs Stevenson's attention veered to the deep voice beside them. "Who is your friend, dear?"

Again with the friend business. For goodness sake, I just met the guy last night.

Charlotte cleared her throat. "This is, Liam Bradly. He was Lincoln's best man."

A cheeky smile worked its way across Mrs Stevenson's face. "Ah, yes, of course. I didn't recognise you out of that gorgeous monkey suit you were wearing at the wedding. I must say you're much cuter up close."

Shocked, Charlotte stifled a gasp. "Mavis! What would George say if he knew you were flirting with a total stranger? A much younger stranger."

"Oh, sweetie," Mavis said with a giggle. "I'm old, not dead. George wouldn't care. In fact, he'd probably be happy my eyesight is working perfectly."

Charlotte's gaze locked on Liam's dumbfounded expression and she lost it. She was soon joined by Mrs Stevenson in fits of laughter.

"I know there will be mostly old fuddy-duddies here, but you're welcome to join the party," she said to both Charlotte and Liam.

Liam was quick to answer. "Actually, Mrs Stevenson, if it's all right with you, I thought I might whisk Charlotte away for an early dinner. I'm new in town and thought she could give me a head's up on the best places to visit while I'm here."

Charlotte stood there in utter bewilderment, unsure of how to react to Liam's offer.

"That sounds like a lovely idea. You two enjoy yourselves," she said, throwing her arms around Charlotte once more. In a soft whisper, she said, "This one looks like fun. Don't waste a minute, dear. Enjoy yourself." She turned and walked off leaving Charlotte stunned.

Cupcakes and Cyanide can be purchased from all good online bookstores or through Gumnut Press.

https://www.gumnutpress.com/